ISBN: 978-0-6922649-4-2

'Walk Witt Me'

'Walk Witt Me'
Volume 1

The Evolution of a young African American Male...

Writing by *Jawan R. Neal*

'Walk Witt Me'

'Walk Witt Me'
Volume 1

The evolution of a young African American male…

I wrote this in hopes to educate as well as inform the urban community, but mostly the young men because it is us that will become future leaders. We have to stop fighting, killing, and destroying our communities.
We're losing our young black males to the streets in a high volume; somebody has to speak-up.

"Without reflection, we lose sight of reality. So always look in the mirror and ask yourself, do you like what you see?"

Jawan R. Neal

Introduction

First and foremost, I'd like to give reverence and thanks to GOD Almighty, my family, and friends. This is an urban novel inspired by my life experiences and the experiences of other urban teens I've encountered. It will show as I traveled through the different stages, how I was able to develop grow mentally and become the person I am today. In the development of these events, characters, and situations, they all motivated me to pause, sit down, and write this novel I'm calling 'Walk Witt Me.'

'Walk Witt Me' as I take this journey of personal discovery and learn life through this process and gain personal strength. There are so many roads one can travel, so much knowledge still to learn, and with the help of our Lord and Savior, I want you to try and reach for the sky as I've been striving toward accomplishing that goal.

Living life as an urban teenager is what I feel passionate about. When we are educating the urban boys, girls, and children there are a multitude of issues on a personal level they face, all while growing up in low-income neighborhoods. In life, we all go through rough times, some may even be unforgettable as teenagers and young adults. There are plenty of up and downs as we going through high school. Sometimes even life altering experiences that take you to certain points in your life can get you thrown off track, but by having strong faith and believing in God, you can get back on the course that He has set for you just as He's doing in my life. From east to west chasing women, money, and hoop dreams only to find in the end that our choices during early stages will dramatically affect the future we've encountered. Therefore, we must make good decisions so you won't continue to walk in circles without making any progress.

The reason I decided to write this book was to serve as a guide to young black males females on how falling off your life course can happen but being able to get back on track through faith and guidance from God you can readjust. I know many of young African American men and women who have ruined their lives by making bad choices. I felt it was my duty and job to write this urban novel and share some of my thoughts as well as experiences. I am very much honored to have traveled the road that I have taken in life. Never will I glorify street activities I have participated in.

But the reality of it all has made me the man I have become today. Talking about my life has always been like stepping on thin ice for me. I was afraid if I did it, the ice would break. I believe I have lived a very unusual and extraordinary life so far and I've had problems like most people. I decided to pour my heart & soul out on paper, speaking as truthfully as possible in hopes that someone could enjoy my life's highs and lows and be able to connect with the message that I'm trying to deliver. So after sitting down at my computer for hours, days, weeks, and even months, I have created this fictional adult novel. The names, cities and events have being altered to protect the innocent.

I would like to recognize a few of the people in spirit, advice and hard work who have inspired and supported me turning my life into a novel, especially the men women in my life who I could talk to about issues and problems as they also served as role models even the educators who come across as negativity or positivity in the process.

I would like to give special recognition to the following persons who have made significant contributions in developing this project. Melvin Lars, Malcolm Stevens, Shanika Carter, and Franklin Fudail.

Contents

Chapter 1

Life as an Urban Teenager

I was standing in my corner office looking out of my glass window, thinking what a beautiful spring morning it was cascading over the city. I had been conducting a final approval of a special project via phone conference with my legal team, as we were closing a new acquisition merger of a former competitor.

Then I noticed a group of youngsters playing ball in a nearby park, and just that quick my mind had a flashback of my early childhood days. When I began this incredible journey during the 1980's in Springfield, Michigan, a medium size urban city located in the western region of the state. Growing up in a small city had its ups and downs.

As I look back, oh, how I miss it. My city was average size but small enough that you felt you knew most everyone who lived there. It was nice because we had our own little community within the city limits. There were no major skyscrapers there but many shopping strips, department stores, mall, lakes, beaches, and plenty of fun activities to do.

A small city comes with many benefits when you grow up in them. These communities allow us as families to become close knit, acquiring a sense of security and familiarity with extended family and friends.

Early on I discovered I had athletic talents and worked diligently to develop my skills, as I became a rising star in basketball, baseball, and football. During this phase of my life, I was remembering when my little brother Kendall and my sister Khalilah were beginning to mimic my every move.

They were developing their skills in athletics and I was proud that they were keeping up the family tradition. I went through a lot of phases and embraced a lot of fads while experiencing life's challenges during the 1980's. In that decade there were a multitude of discoveries, explorations, tragedies, and newfound interests in sports, music and life in general.

My parents were very proud, loving, supportive and industrious as they provided a great home for Khalilah, Kendall, and me. As a family we enjoyed spending time going to the movies, bowling and living life.

There were many challenges, disappointments and opportunities endured by our family. My parents were the average everyday African-American, middle class family. My mother was employed by the Springfield Public School District as a schoolteacher, and Pops was a construction worker at a local construction company.

Unfortunately, my family, primarily my father, weathered a series of storms with long periods of unemployment during the Reagan and Bush eras. His participation in the labors union played a significant role in his constant unemployment due to the union picketing and boycotting to seek job security at a fair financial compensation.

My mother instilled in us family values that included being successful in school and attending church. Pop's was also about those values, but he was a real man's man who loved the outdoors and all that it had to offer such as, hunting, fishing, and all sports.

He never pushed us to play sports, however it seemed to be a part of us as we grew and developed interest and curiosity causing us to gravitate toward those kinds of activities.

Now these were some of the best times I had growing up in the 80's. Our family was music lovers who enjoyed new and old vocal artists. I idolized Michael Jackson, NWA, New Edition and LL Cool J's "I Need Love." I thought I was LL Cool J for a few years when he came out on the scene, until I was on to the next celebrity.

One time I thought of myself as Michael Jackson during the Thriller album era. I would dress-up like Michael Jackson and perform a live concert for my family at my grandparent's house while my family was sitting around playing cards and enjoying life. It was my belief my family would never let me live that down.

The world of technology was upon us as Apple and IBM introduced new lines of revolutionary computers along with video game systems, Atari. I was one of the first kids in the hood with an Atari 2600, Nintendo (1985) and Sega Genesis (1989). My passion for fashion began to pique at this time. My wardrobe included biking shorts, Used and Guess jeans.

And I can't forget MC Hammer pants, how could I ever forget these? Sports team's apparel and figures were also emerging at this time: Air Michael Jordan, Dr. J, Walter Payton, Michael Tyson, Wayne Gretzky, Magic Johnson, The Detroit Bad Boys, Chicago Bulls, Chicago Bears (1985), Detroit Red Wings, L.A. Lakers, and Chicago Cubs. I had a wall full of these paraphernalia in my bedroom.

During this very exciting period in my development we were also dealt a very bad hand with the "discovery" of a very brutal, debilitating and deadly STD known as HIV/AIDS, which had become a major epidemic in our communities and across the country.

The negative onslaught continued as both legal and illegal drugs, and substance abusers caused family disasters in epidemic proportions as it destroyed inner-city families like mine. Also during this period, several different drugs were gaining popularity among inner-city youths, namely marijuana and crack cocaine, and no one can forget the effects of alcohol on our communities and the number one used drug.

Rock cocaine a.k.a. CRACK was by far one of the most addicting drugs out there. It's been over taking America's inner cities since the early 80's. Heroin was also making a comeback. Alcohol and marijuana were still very popular in the hood and suburbs. There are some very distinctive differences in how those drugs were viewed and how substance abuse was seen between the less fortunate classes in comparison to the middle and upper class communities. The rich man's drug of choice is powder cocaine. The poor folks prefer rock cocaine. Alcohol was popular in both classes but also in different preferences. The upper and middle-class teenagers seem to want to experiment more with designer or new age drugs. The reason that there is so much media hype about drug abuse among the poor is because of the great disparity when it involved sentencing.

Even courts in our area gave stiffer sentences for persons convicted of distributing crack cocaine than they did for those distributing powered cocaine, and they were actually the same drug just in different forms shit was crazy. A person could get a higher sentence if caught with smaller amounts crack cocaine, than a person caught with larger amounts of powdered cocaine.

This is not an accurate stat but the way I viewed it was African-American communities account for 80 percent of all federal crack distributors. Unfair sentencing shows how the judicial system levied harder penalties on blacks for drug violations than whites. The upper and middle-class teens did their fair share of drugs with far less life-changing consequences and very little or no jail time. The reason I have mentioned this situation is because these were the obstacles I had to overcome to make it out of the hood as a young, African-American male in the 80's. Those were tough times for black folks, because of the depression and the financial challenges that our communities faced. Things I'm speaking about hit close to home. I had uncles, cousins, other family and friends that were negatively affected by unfair and unjust provisions of the law.

We also dealt with the lack of jobs and economic stability in the community itself, causing industries to shut down and move out of our community with great regularity.

Also during the 80's we were graced with many rising movie stars and movie directors, such as John Singleton, Spike Lee, Eddie Murphy, Phylicia Rashad, Red Foxx, Janet Jackson, and Richard Pryor.

These artists' amazed audiences through their expertise as thespians, comedians, and writers because of their ability to bring on the public stage the urban lifestyle and inject many of the nuances into the mainstream of the American medium. I remember that Pryor presented the popular comedy "Which Way Is Up". The urban community as well as the world marveled at George Lucas's "Star Wars" series.

Various movies premiered changing the face and texture of the film industry, including Robo-Cop starring Peter Weller, "The Terminator" starring Arnold Schwarzenegger, "E.T. the Extra-Terrestrial" with Drew Barrymore, and "Back to the Future" with Christopher Lloyd and Michael J. Fox. These were all box-office smashes in the 80s. There were also other memorable movies like "Police Academy", "Breakin", "Krush Groove", "The Fish That Saved Pittsburgh", and "Enter the Dragon". How many of us can remember sitting back on a summer day drinking a glass of Kool-Aid or an Italian Icy watching "Return of The A-Team", "Transformers", "Go-Bots" or "G.I. Joe?"

There were many movies and television shows that reflected the American culture at that time and had a tremendous motivation and impact on teenagers during that era. Several television shows and movies that addressed societal trends and problems such as murder, rape, racism, and on a less serious note, parties, shopping, and sports, that deserved serious consideration by the public and the media.

There were television shows like "Save By The Bell" and "Beverly Hills 90210" that tried give an accurate portrayal of the life of the typical well off American teenagers growing up in the 80's and 90's but this still wasn't the case for the African-American viewers like myself.

Though these teens were faced with average problems of being a youth, we in the urban community had totally opposite problems to deal with just trying to survive in the hood. You could tell that the producers of this shows attempted to integrate many real-life situations into there shows. By doing this, they were suggesting to the audience situations that happened to be geared toward teenagers and what the characters did in the shows was the ideal way of dealing with these types of situations. However, Bill Cosby created "The Cosby Show, a depiction of a financially stable African-American family where both the father and the mother were professionals, a doctor and lawyer, respectively.

The show dealt with instilling family values in their children. Cosby also created "A Different World", which featured stories about young African American students attending a historical black college and how college life was for young blacks coming up in the mid 80's. The show also dealt with the many challenges, disappointments, and successes of young men and women of color who were educating themselves on this beautiful college campus. "Good Times" was the opposite of "The Cosby Show". They were an African-American family that was engulfed in "hard times" in the 70's in the ghetto of a Chicago housing project.

It reflected constant unemployment of the family patriarch and his ultimately leaving the family to be headed by the matriarch of the family.

Then there was "The Jefferson's", a story about a black business man who started his own small dry cleaning business in the neighborhood, eventually turning it into a chain of cleaners all on the south side of the city. After he "made it" he moved to the east side to a deluxe apartment in the sky.

One of my all-time favorite sitcoms was "Sanford & Son" which was about a father and his son who owned a little junk business in the ghetto of Watts, California. This was a sitcom that my father and I would watch downstairs in our basement after he put in a long day at work.

This was going on while my mother, sister and brother would be upstairs, they playing with their toys, and mom would be cooking a late dinner. Right after we watched a few black sitcoms my father would flip to the Piston's game. I really admired Isaiah Thomas, he was one of my favorite basketball players of all time outside of Dr. J and Air Michael Jordan. This was how most evenings would be in the Macklemore's immediate family household. For me, this was a complete night until my mom, the teacher, would always ask that one question most kids hate. "Kendrick, do you have any homework?" It would always be right when I was deep into a level or trying to master something on my Nintendo or Sega Genesis game systems. I always had the same two answers every time. "Yeah momma, I didn't have any today" or "Yeah momma, I did it all at school early."

My mother would then respond, "Ok Kendrick, if I find out you didn't do it or if you did have some that's going to be your butt!!!" Then I would continue to play my game until it was time for me to take a bath and get in the bed for the night.

I could never go straight to sleep so my pops would always come in the room and tell Kendall and me a bedtime story and then go tuck in Khalilah as well. We both liked it when he told us the one about the three little pigs and the big bad wolf, but it wasn't the regular version of the story, it was my pop's version of the story. Instead of using the three little pigs, he would use three players from the NBA like Isaiah Thomas, Air Michael Jordan, and Magic Johnson as the three pigs and either Charles Barkley, Karl Malone, or Hakeem Olajuwon as the big bad wolf. I loved these bedtime stories until I was like 12 years old.

After age 12, I started telling Kendall these stories at night. He enjoyed them just as we did when our pops told them to us. My family and I enjoyed spending time with each other. We loved going to the drive-in during the summer months, and loved fishing and hunting. My family was good for throwing cookouts, which most of the neighborhood would attend. There were two-on-two basketball games that my dad and I would always win. You see, Pops could hoop in his day and I was turning into an exceptional player myself. I was practicing day in and day out on my game so I loved when it was time to hoop.

Life for me in the late 80's and early 90's was starting to be all about sports and girls, I loved them both and I think the love was equal. Just as I became the preteen athlete, I also became the ladies' man as well as all that came with the territory. Besides sports and females, I also enjoyed playing video games with my best friend Orlando.

We would play the game for hours on in any given day. Orlando was my man. I spent so much of my childhood with him. We would probably hang out 12 to 15 hours a day. We were like brothers from a different mother. We had other friends as well like Cedric, Kyle, and Quintrell, sometimes called Trell.

For the most part, though, when you saw me you knew Orlando wasn't too far behind. Orlando and I would talk about everything, we shared lots of preteen stories and childhood memories that we would take with us on into our teenage years and throughout our lives. I can really say he was definitely a great friend that never wanted nor asked for anything more than just being a friend, that's why he will always be one of my best friends for a long time to come.

Wow, it's funny to me how mischievous I was as a teenager. "The teen years were the best days of your life" is an old saying that I always heard adults use. Then there was, "What I wouldn't give to be your age again." Then my all-time favorite is, "If I knew then, what I know now, I would have done things differently." Little did they know that such sayings would make teens rebel and try to find their own way.

As I stated before, my mother was a schoolteacher and my father was in construction, so I guess this was the ideal family setting, but I wasn't a regular teenage boy. I was sneaky and already sexually active and girl crazy by this time in my life.

Sports kept me grounded. At this stage in my life, both my parents and my teachers were only just beginning to understand but refused to acknowledge that I had some problems. I was beginning to let out my frustration and anger, and I had a lot of it too. I was angry because my parents split up and this was still bothering me greatly although they were back together. I still felt uncomfortable in some kind of way, but again sports were an escape.

One of the things I did excel in was playing sports. I took all of my anger and vented on the sports playing fields in all arenas, using sports as a form of relief. My family and I were sitting around on the porch. It was a beautiful sunny Saturday morning in Springfield, Michigan. There was a cool breeze blowing, the birds were chirping, the dogs were barking. There was the sound of children playing and the sounds of traffic heard in the background. It was an all-around beautiful day in the neighborhood. Our neighbor Mr. Woods was mowing his lawn a few doors down. The brothers at the neighborhood church were trimming the hedges. It was the end of summer going into my seventh grade year and I was trying to prepare myself for attending junior high school.

The start of my junior high school year was very interesting because it all began the summer of '89. I had just finished elementary school that June and it was now time for little league baseball.

This was my last year I could play little league and I was highly anticipating the start of this season. It was June 7th and the first day of practice was on the 15th and I couldn't wait, so I came up with an idea to start rounding up the guys to begin playing every day until the first day of practice began.

I figured since we won the championship last season we should practice so we could win again for my final year. I got on my Huffy mountain bike and went over Donovan Thompson house to get him so he could help me round up the guys. He was one of the three captains. I said lets go get Nick because he's the other captain, so we headed to Nicholas Daily's crib. Nick had two big-ass pit-bull dogs, which were becoming popular in the hood. When we got there neither me nor Donovan wanted to go to the door, but luckily his little brother was in the front yard playing and we asked him was Nick home. He replied, "Yeah, he in there" and then took off running like a bat out of hell to get him.

Nick came out with his shirt off and said, "What up, y'all?"

"Man we about to play some baseball. Grab your shit and come on." I responded. He went back in the house and after 10 minutes he came riding around the corner on his bike.

"Who should we go get next?" I asked.

"Let's go get Charles because I ain't playing catcher this year," Nick said.

"Bet!" Donovan said. It was funny because I knew the real reason nobody wanted to be the back catcher was because they said I threw too hard. So we traveled to the south side to get Lamont and the other Donovan, Donovan Black. We were all riding back to Jackie Robinson Park to practice and Trell was riding up at the same time.

"Yo Trell, you must got my message?" I said.

"Yeah, that's why I'm here."

So we had most of the starters back together and practiced without a coach till it got dark, and we continued to do so every day until the 15th of June. The first day of practice was funny, we were running wind sprints and laps, and hitting the ball. I had just come off of a 14 home run season and was very pumped up about the batting practice that day, but I hit the ball terribly all practice and was very upset with myself. When it was my turn to pitch I threw the ball as hard as I could throw it so no one would hit the ball.

16

I knew I had the heat going. Coach Golden decided to sit me on the bench and said, "You're acting like a broad." There were about 30 kids that tried out that day. We had so many guys because we were the defending champs so there were more people than ever trying to make this 15 man roster. I loved and enjoyed playing for Coach Golden, plus he was my godfather and my dad's best friend. Coach Golden was a 5'8", 155-pound, dark-skinned Army (Vietnam) veteran and a great baseball coach who got the best from his player as well as his teams. He also provided the players that didn't have fathers a true father figure. You could go to him for anything that was within reason, that is. Practices were over and cuts had been made.

It was two days before the season opener against none other than Franklin's Corner Store, our number one rival and I was ready to defend our championship. We went on to finish the season 19-2 and once again won the East League Championship for the second year in a row.

Also that year my city's all-star team qualified for the Little League World Series by winning the state's title.

We beat 15 teams in the state tournament to move to the regional tournaments, led by yours truly. During the state qualifying rounds I led the team in every category. I was batting 550. I had 15 home runs, 35 RBI's, 47 stolen bases, and 77 strikeouts in that state run.

We didn't do as well in the regional tournament. We lost the first two games and that ended our Little League World Series dreams. It was one of my earliest childhood experiences that I will always cherish. Even though we came up short of our goal, we still went farther than any team from our side of the state had gone, plus we were state champs if nothing else.

Baseball season came and went now it was time to prepare for junior high football and prepare for junior high school itself. It was the end of the summer of '89 and I had a blast. I went and visited my uncle and cousins in Dover Creek, Michigan for the last two weeks of my summer vacation. My cousins and I would do all types of things like basketball, football, swimming, and just plain chilling.

Outside of the King family cookouts on the 4th of July, going to Dover Creek was always a great way to close out the summer. One Sunday afternoon my parents pulled up to Uncle Fishburn's house and that's when I knew that my summer was over, because tomorrow morning it was back to school. It was the start of the school year and they already had the boys football and girls basketball signup sheets posted all around the building.

The junior high building was a large, sprawling building that covered the whole block. It was two stories tall with a new recently built section and a cafeteria that doubled as an all-purpose room.

The Labor Day holiday was over, and school started with a blast. The hallways were long, reminding you of caves. My friends and I arrived earlier that morning. The teachers were there to greet us. Who wanted to be bothered with them? We went to the bathroom to get our game plan on.

While in the bathroom with my G.W. Carver crew, we ran into Charles, Mark, Bryan, Cory, and Reynard along with their crews from the other elementary schools. With a quick meet and greet, we all knew each other from participating in the elementary league sports.

Now we were all at junior high. Some of us had been the stars at our neighborhood schools. Now it was time to claim turf at junior high. Just after this small conference, I emerged as the new unofficial leader of the 7th grade boy's class.

The bell rang and everybody scattered trying to figure out where our homeroom classes were. It was the start of the school year and the signup forms were posted all over the building. I knew I had to sign up but I was kind of scared because there were some very big 8th graders that had played on last year's team. This made me a little nervous. Even though I knew I was still one of the school's best athletes, I was also one of the smallest players. During lunchtime I decided to sign my name. Bump it, I said to myself. I'll do it and see what happens. By the end of the day, the secretary announced over the intercom that all the guys who had signed the list were to show up outside on the practice field.

We all came out and met the coaches. I would estimate that there were about 50 guys that had signed up. But as I looked around I knew there were going to be a lot of these guys that were going to quit. I could just see it in most of their faces as the coaches were telling us what they expected and how hard we had to work to meet those expectations.

One week later the final cuts were made and the official team roster was posted. On that list there were 41 names. Then I saw it, number 10, Kendrick Macklemore. I was very confident that I would make the team but I won't lie I was a little nervous all weekend because there were some really good 8th grade players. Everybody wanted to get an Eric Dickerson's facemask but that only went to the best players. We couldn't wait to see who the coaches were going to assign those facemasks, including the jersey numbers we would get. In those days it was not unusual to receive the leftover, hand-me-downs from the high school varsity, junior varsity, and even the freshman teams.

When I reflect back, much of that equipment would be considered dangerous, non-usable and really should be discarded. In the suburban-outlying community most, if not all, of that kind of leftover equipment would have been thrown away. To us, we were just happy to have equipment and uniforms to play the game. There were only 15 Dickerson's facemasks and only five 7th graders got them. I was one of them, plus I got the number 12 jersey which NFL superstar quarterback Randall Cunningham of the Philadelphia Eagles wore. I played quarterback (QB) at this point. I didn't know if I was going to be the starter or not but I did know that I was very happy with my jersey.

Now with our full gear and a week behind us, it appeared that I was going to be the starter. There were only two 7th graders to crack the starting lineup on offense my center and myself. We won six out of 12 games, which were three more games than they won the year before. As a first year junior high starter QB I was extremely excited. During the season I started dating one of the baddest chicks in my school. She was a tall dark skinned, very attractive, thick, young lady that could pass for an 18 year old. She was also was very mature for her age. October 30, 1990, the day before Halloween, was the day my trouble all started. This rainy morning I received a note from her about our relationship and the note read: ***Dear Kendrick,***

I do really like you but this relationship has to go to the next level because all my friends are doing things I want to do with my boyfriend, like kissing and sitting with their boyfriends at lunch. I'm being left out, so if you aren't willing to step up to the plate then we're going to have to end this relationship because there are several dudes that's trying to get at me and they are willing to meet my expectations. Plus, I heard you were talking to Delaney. If this is not true I am waiting by the girl's gym for my kiss to seal the deal!!!
Sincerely Yours.
Laurie Gregory

Since I wasn't ready to meet her request I didn't go see her at the girl's gym. Yep you guessed it, she dropped me like a bad habit. I was a little sad but relieved because I was not yet sure of my sexual abilities, so I was a single man again. This time I was looking for someone who was more on my level as far as how I viewed dating at that time in my life.

Then there was Carmen, a caramel complexioned, young lady. This was my "love at first sight" person. The first time I saw her I was impressed. She was built like a high school student. She had a big booty and nice breasts to be in 7th grade. To a hormone raging 13-year-old this was just too much.

Carmen and I started going steady right after the National Honors Society party for all the students that made the honor roll from the first period. It started when I asked her if I could walk her home and she said, "Yeah, that's okay with me." We walked and talked all the way to her house, which was about 14 or 15 blocks from the school. The conversation was so good that we didn't notice how quickly we had gotten to her street.

I gave her a friendly hug, we exchanged telephone numbers, and she went in the house and I left. For weeks, even months, after this new relationship, Carmen and I were the perfect junior high couple. We did everything from walk to class, walk home, and talk on the phone for hours on every day. You know, early teen stuff.

My favorite time of the year was upon us. You guessed it, basketball season. We had 7th grade boys basketball tryouts, which would last for two days. The first day went well. I was my usual self, kicking butt. It was one of those days where everything was working. Day two, unlike day one, was a day I just couldn't do anything right.

This day will always stand out because on this day I got my greatest reality check. I was cut from the team. I was not cut because of my inability to play the game but for having a negative attitude and poor sportsmanship. This was a very hard time for me.

I had never gone through a school year without playing basketball. For most people this would not have seemed like a big thing, but for a person that's a real athlete it can be a major setback and it could affect you for a lifetime. It started affecting my grades and my classroom behavior, and everyone was wondering why.

After suffering through the next two months and my 7th grade team going 11-1 without me, I was not a happy camper. Hoop season had come and went and I was still angry and jealous because I missed my favorite sport. Then to add insult on top of injury, the team actually did great without me.

I can't even lie, this was a very tough time for me because after each workout or pickup game I played I cried like a baby whenever I was alone. During that time I felt terribly by myself. For a teenage athlete, even with good people advising me, this was still a big blow to my ego even with the determination I had within myself. For the first time I had been knocked down and it was now time to pick myself up and really see what I was made out of.

Chapter 2

Growing Up in The 90's

I had to form a plan from the things I knew as well gleaned from the point of things that Kenny Holiday, the ex-standout, told me. Just as the school year ended one of my dad's friends who was a local ex-high-school/college standout basketball player gave me some advice that stuck with me forever. All that summer I was determined to be ready for my 8th grade year. I dedicated my summer vacation to becoming a better player, student, and also a better young man.

That summer I shot 2,000 jump shots a day and played in over 200 AAU games, team camps, and pickup games. I would jog 10 miles and do countless wind sprints along with dribbling drills daily. I had to make sure I proved myself to the coach and to those cats that played on the team without me. I was, for the first time in my life, the odd man out.

When I look back upon that time of my life and look back at some of the lessons I learned, I realized that your directions could be changed when you come up against someone who has greater authority over your actions. Life is not always what you think it is sometimes. When you make a mistake, you have to be willing to change and adjust your direction. There are times in life when you realize that the choices you make while you are young can have life altering consequences and outcomes.

Even though the lessons and understandings were there, it still took me a while to be able to incorporate those lessons into my playing lifestyle. I still had a lot of growing up to do. See I knew that it wasn't my skills or my inability to play the game, and it even took me a few weeks and a discussion with Coach Littleton to understand the importance of this sportsmanship bullshit. While in my youth I didn't think it had nothing to do with hooping, but I guess it was more important than I thought. I had to make sure I paid closer attention to it next season as well as throughout my career.

Imagine this if you would, it was a great day in the neighborhood and it was time for my family's 5th reunion with the sounds of Will Smith's "Summertime" playing in the background. "Summer, summer, summertime time to sit back and unwind. Here it is the groove slightly transformed, just a bit of a break from the norm, just a little somethin' to break the monotony of all that hardcore dance that has gotten to be a little bit out of control it's cool to dance but what about the groove that soothes that moves romance. Give me a soft subtle mix and if ain't broke then don't try to fix it and think of the summers of the past adjust the base and let the alpine blast. Pop in my CD and let me run a rhyme and put your car on cruise and lay back cause this is summertime!"

It was middle of the summer of '91 I had just turned 13. We had not had a family reunion in a few years. It was the first one had in the Midwest in about 10 years. Some of the other family members had already arrived a day early and had checked into their hotel rooms. That evening we were meeting for dinner at a local restaurant. It turned out to be pleasant, for the most part. The food was good, and I saw a few of my cousins that I hadn't seen in years. All of my girl cousins huddled around a table by themselves and talked girl talk, boys, and sex. I'm sure the typical teenage stuff, and us guys did likewise in our private conversations. The first day of the reunion was an important time to set the tone.

My mother and a few of our older cousins made a place for people to register, pay remaining fees, get nametags and so forth. My Uncle Hollywood had some activities planned, such as icebreakers and mixers, to help these family members get better acquainted or renew old friendships.

Remember that some attendees were first timers, spouses, new cousins, long lost family members, etc., so he made sure that they felt welcome and appreciated. Looking back, sometime I was surprised at the talent that my older family members displayed during those events. Many activities were planned for us and a number of my family members enjoyed the swimming pool, tennis courts, softball, soccer, flag football and my favorite, of course, basketball.

While playing some of the games my people would always tell me to take it easy. "It's only a game." Because when I played, I played to win at all cost.

K.P. Pepper Park was a beautiful outdoor setting in downtown Springfield, where we held our 5th family reunion. To everyone's surprise, more than 100 people showed up. During the night there were firecrackers and campfires, and this was a delight to the kids.

This was a great event during this time of the summer for me and the rest of my family.

All weekend my pop's reminded me about working on my sportsmanship. Man, I just can't escape this sportsmanship thing, I guess it goes a long way.

Also, during my teenage years, I went through major changes with my body that needed to be explained. I was too ashamed to ask anyone, though. So at the beginning of puberty my hormones started racing and I began to experience sexual urges. It wasn't something anyone prepared me for, and I couldn't control it. Going by what my sex ed teacher told me, it's a natural function of the body and has been since the beginning of time. During that summer I had an experience that I'll never forget. On July 21, 1991, while chilling over my Aunt Rachel's house one night, I made the fatal mistake of getting drunk for the first time in my life. I was just a bad ass and I can remember on this night watching my aunts, mother, and their friends drink as they got ready for the club.

Soon as they hit the door I went straight to the kitchen and picked up where they left off. I began to drink right out of the bottle of Five O' Clock Gin they left on the table. There were only about two shots that remained in the bottle but I got tipsy off those two shots.

Meanwhile, my little brother and cousin watched me in awe as I sat at the kitchen table like a grown man sipping and puffing on a cigarette. About 30 minutes passed and there was a knock at the door, and it was my Cousin Denise's best friends. They were both 9th grade girls like my cousin and I could tell that the light skinned one was feeling me. I was drunk and had a sexual urge but had never been with an older girl before.

Under the circumstances, this was an unfamiliar situation for me. They kicked it in my cousin's room for a few hours, then the light skinned very well shaped girl named Sequoia came out in the living room where my little cousin Brock, my little brother Kendall, and I were. They were sleeping on the floor and I was on the couch. She waited till Denise and their other friend went to sleep and that's when she came out of the room and laid on the smaller couch.

"Kendrick, are you sleep?" she asked. "Naw, I'm up, I can't go to sleep for shit," I responded. "Then come over here, and bring that cover." I quickly got up and went over to her. In about two minutes we started kissing. In my head I was thinking what I do next.

Damn, I've never gone this far! So as we continued to kiss as she began to reach in my shorts, grab my teenage dick, and began to stroke it. I had never felt this feeling I was getting from my dick before. So I just copied what she did to me. I stuck my hand in her pajama pants and found my hand touching her pubic hairs. I reached a little further and I found her pussy, it was very wet down there.

This and the liquor I had drunk was enough to have me ready to do it but the strange thing was I had never done it before. I was like, "Fuck it this might be my first and only time. What the hell?" Right then she ripped down my shorts and boxers. I lifted up her shirt and unclipped her bra. She started to rub her now bare pussy up and down my thigh while I was playing with her tits. She started to play with my balls and I couldn't concentrate. I grabbed her around the hips and pulled her on top of me and started to bounce her up and down. She started to moan but we had to keep quiet. I kept her bouncing for over 10 minutes then she started making more noise.

"Everybody sleep don't wake them up!" I said. She had pussy juice running all over the place. I started to fuck her harder but she seemed to be able to take it. Then she whispered to me, "Cum, cum, cum," so I did all over my aunt's couch. At first I thought my dick was broke because I had never saw this white stuff ever come out my dick before. "Wow, my first real sexual encounter," was what I was thinking.

When it was over, she said it was the best she ever had, and since it was my first time I was proud of myself. I did keep meeting up with her at my aunt's house on a regular basis after that. My aunts and mother returned home unexpectedly but luckily they didn't catch us. We continued to get together from time to time to have sex but after a few months it faded out. One thing it did for me was increase my confidence. I began to go after the girls that I once was scared of a brief time before.

This year's Springfield Air Show seemed different from previous ones in several ways. The United States Military was introducing during the air show the world famous Blue-Angels Flying Squad along with presenting one of the new Stealth Bombers, which had never been revealed at the previous Springfield Air Shows. The events were more focused on collaboration as opposed to previous years. This year was much more about the different military branches coming together as teams. There were more joint flights as opposed to the individual performance of the previous years.

The team efforts were unbelievable to see. Me, some of my friends, and teammates got to see them up close while we worked on the flight grounds, as people enjoyed the event. There were dynamic acrobatic displays and flying performances that were breathtaking. A smoke display was added with the flying team's performance.

That summer we experienced what it meant to be volunteers to an event as we raised money in support of our local pony league baseball team.

On the last day of the air show it was one of the hottest days during the summer, as well as a day where we had the most fun. I really got a chance to be a kid and just let my hair down at this event. Me and my crew of volunteers managed to get our hands on bottled water, extra sodas, and snacks. And oops…we probably forgot to pay for it! On top of that, we somehow managed to have fun with the pilots and airport staff as if they were regular people just like us.

A big water-balloon fight was started, we sprayed each other with water hoses, splashed buckets of water on each other and just had fun while we cooled down. It was wonderful because we had an opportunity to meet and talk in a very informal environment and restricted area with some of these pilots who had been flying these outstanding airplanes.

We all felt like this was one of the best summers ever. Naturally, I got my collection of girls' telephone numbers and some of my friends ended up with a case of grape soda. We had those for several days after the event as we laughed about that experience. Yep, that was one of the best summers ever.

I enjoyed all of the things that the 80's had to offer me, although they were tough times for my family and me. My parents seemed to always make a way when things got bad. They were two hard working, African-Americans whose main goal was to make life for my sister, brother and myself as easy as possible. When I reflect on the 80's, life was not all that bad and seemed easier. At age 13 I didn't have a care in the world.

To me it was all about playing sports, chasing girls, and just being with friends. I was just completing my 7th grade year of school and going into the 8th grade, which was my reality. It was about my crew Orlando, Kyle, Cedric and me. We use to do all the things 8th grade boys did. That summer we played basketball in my yard and also Kyle's yard from sun up to sun down. We would just go at it, and we would also go to the parks and play baseball, football, etc. I was very fond of the parts of the day when we went to the corner-store.

That's where all the girls hung out, and at this stage in my life my hormones were totally out of control. I can remember that everything I did in this period of my life was because of females and being popular.

Though Cedric and I came to junior high from elementary with the reputation of being good in sports, eventually I surpassed him when it came to athletics' so everybody wanted to challenge me or be like me in some regard.

I'm trying not to sound cocky or arrogant but in my mind I had turned into the next Malik Samson on the football field and Xavier McKinney on the basketball court. I was on my way in sports so I tried to be the best at everything I did. I just took on the same attitude with females too.

I wanted to be the best out of my group, just like I wanted to be the best athlete. Out of the crew I was still the closest to Orlando, although Cedric and I played most of the sports together. Cedric and I were also cousins, but I still had a better bond with Orlando. Now, Orlando had the skills to be good in sports he just didn't have the confidence. At 13, Orlando was 5'6" and around 158 lbs., which is a good size for a football player getting ready for 8th grade-ball next year. On the other hand, Cedric was about 5'7," 160 pounds, and had all the confidence in the world so he was pumped up like me for tryouts.

The first day of tryouts I got to the school early to lift weights and run some wind sprints before everyone got there. I didn't even notice the head, varsity coach observing me because I was so into my workout routine. He then called me over.

"Son, your name is Macklemore right?"

"Yes sir, Kendrick Macklemore," I responded.

"So, what are you doing here so early?"

"I just wanted to be ready for this season, coach."

"Are you playing varsity ball or JV next year?"

"I just want to play. I'll play where ever y'all need me sir!"

"Ok make sure you practice hard this summer because you still have to do the other workouts before the real practice begins."

This was the beginning of my legendary high school career before I ever stepped on the high school gridiron field. First, I had to get through the summertime and workouts before the actual first tryouts began in Springfield, MI. On September 7, 1990, after we had been practicing hard all summer, the games had finally begun.

During the last three weeks football practice had put over 250 athletes at eight Springfield public middle schools into action. We were tired and sore but became more fit each day. This year the league welcomed the Mount Vernon Pilot School and Riverbank. Our returning schools included Cedarwood High, Armstrong High, Sunset High, Green Run, and the Springfield West Prep.

We played a 12-week season ending with a championship game on November 12th. The season began with so much anticipation with the new additions. My community was very pleased to have our own superintendent making the introductory speech. "We are happy to welcome two more teams to our league this year," said Dr. Jerry Henderson, Springfield's School Superintendent.

"Through the generosity of our donors and our continued fundraising we are able to expand this conference. It's exciting to have 60 more student athletes on the field this fall to participate and we are hopeful this is a trend we can continue in the years to come."

Some of the other coaches from a few of the schools followed Dr. Jerry Henderson with brief speeches of their own. And last, my head coach took the podium.

"We had 50 students try out and 12 returning players," said Chuck Morton, my eighth-grade coach at Springfield Junior High. "Last year the majorities of our players were playing organized football for the first time and gave it their all. We were pleased with the effort our players showed on and off the field.

With our returning players and the enthusiasm of our new team members we are looking forward to a very exciting year. I've coached a number of sports teams over the years and I am glad to have this opportunity to work with my students at Springfield Junior High.

While we have a solid basketball program, football gives us a chance to involve more student athletes that are new to organized sports. Of our roster, 20 student's athletes have never played organized football before. And my staff takes this as a challenge, as well as an honor, and we give them the skills to grow into young men."

Two weeks before the first game, one of our assistant coaches and defensive coordinators, Leon Barnett, got into a serious car accident removing him of his love and passion for us as well as the game of football. This took a toll on the whole program because he pushed that mental toughness and held that aggressive spirit. I once remember him saying,

"If you see me fighting a bear, help the bear." To us he represented a drive, a focus and a determination that we would need sometimes in a tough game to help us get over the top. And now to find out he wasn't gonna be with us for the remainder of the season was a major blow.

So my football team had to come together through this very rough incident that had come upon us. The next few weeks of our lives would be some of the best and worst times of my life that I could remember. Even without Coach Barnett there were other issues that affected our team.

Like, after hearing that story about one of my teammate's Toby's sister. I couldn't believe it when I got the phone call that a few high school cheerleaders had been killed by a drunk driver the night before our first game. They were coming home from a party at a friend's house. I was filled with anger, rage, and a deep sense of loss for my friend and our team within a short period of time.

Being team captain, I felt it was my responsibility to rally all the players together and challenge them to help make this year a perfect season for us, and that we should dedicate this to Toby's sister and Coach Barnett.

This experience touched all of our lives and really hit home. We were an extremely close football team. We recognized that Head Coach Chuck Morton was really going to need me to step up my game. It was such a hard moment for us as a team. But through teamwork and perseverance we felt that we would definitely make it. Going for a perfect season and honoring my teammates' sister and our coach we were up for the challenge. We began our journey to this perfect season we had aimed for. It was a beautiful fall day in Springfield, MI.

The sun was shining, and the leaves had turned a bright orange and brown from the autumn air. I must say this was a great day for the season-opener. The time was 2:30 p.m. and the beginning of the game was only 30 minutes away now. The fans and viewers had started filling up the bleachers for the opening kickoff.

The national anthem was played, there was a coin toss, and we took the ball first. I took the kickoff 74 yards for the game's first touchdown score.

Everybody knew the game was on. In this game against Riverbank, we dominated from the opening kickoff to the ending play.

While never letting off the gas, this turned into a blowout with the final score ending 48-12. I completed the game with one kickoff return, three touchdown passes, 140 yards passing, 67 rushing, seven tackles, and two interceptions. This was definitely a statement game for me trying to show my team I was dead serious about our team goals.

We went on to complete the magical season, 16-0 and one game left against Springfield West Prep who had a powerhouse football program. You guessed it, the opportunity to honor our team commitment versus one of the area's best programs, along with a special appearance from Coach Barnett who was on the sidelines for the first time all season. Although he was in a wheelchair, he was on the sidelines none-the- less.

During our first conference league championship game, it was a great beginning half. The team played well and I even did some great things in this game, but Springfield West Prep just overpowered us in the end with a score of 60-21.

After that brutal loss and falling short of our team goals, along with the hopes of a perfect season, it seemed as we couldn't be beaten. We were the team of destiny and it all came to a crushing end that Saturday evening.

The 8th grade basketball season had rolled around once again, and both the 7th and 8th grade boys' teams were expected to have successful seasons.

My team had six players returning with all five starters from the previous year's team, and there was fresh talent in the 7th grade, as well, ready to challenge the better players. Our boys' team consisted of Reynard, Bryan, Anthony, Mark, Cory, and Charles, who all played on the 7th grade squad. The 7th grade boys included William, Jermaine, Demetric, and Eugene who were new students to Springfield Junior High School.

They were excited to begin their careers as the Knights. The team, as well as myself, had high expectations for the year, with the addition of Reynard and me as the team's unofficial leader. I expected this team to match and exceed what they did last season. I was pumped up and well prepared for this season with all the practice and hard work I put in during the off season. I was expecting to have a great year. I could hardly wait for the first game against Armstrong and every game we would play this year for that matter.

The season opener for us was hyped with so many expectations with the two top teams squaring off in the first game of the year. It was a Thursday evening game time. Everyone was talking about it all day in school and I was very nervous as to what I might do in it.

Yep, me Kendrick, the kid with all the confidence in the world was scared to play in an 8th grade basketball game. It was almost game time, my mindset was cold, deep, dark, anxious, and a still little bit nervous at this time. I was preparing myself for the most crucial game of my 8th grade career, my first game. I turned off the water and headed back to my locker to put on my game jersey on for the first time this year.

I paused and daydreamed about all of this I had missed last season. Then it was broken when I heard my manz, Charles, yell from down at the other end, "Kendrick, what the hell are you doing? You have to get ready to go!"

"Oh yeah" I responded. As we walked up the stairs through the dark hallway in front of us, I was thinking to myself about what would I do, how would I react, and what was in store for me during this game. The game began and after the jump ball all the emotion quickly went away as I was bringing the ball up the floor getting us into our offensive sets. They kind of defended it well, so I faked right and then went left and pulled up for a 15-foot jump shot. Nothing but net! I got it started, game on!

"Kendrick for three!" our home announcer Craig Holmes yelled over the PA system. I sure was lighting up the gym tonight for my first junior high school boys basketball game.

"WOAH! That makes 45 points and seven three-pointers!"

"That's right, Craig. This kid has been unstoppable all night!" his partner said to him following their second team timeout. My team was ahead of the Armstrong Gophers 87-80 with two minutes remaining.

"Get over here!" screamed my head coach Melvin James to us. Coach James was a living legend in Springfield. As a teenager, James had two homes, Springfield High School's gym, Great Value Park, the capital of street basketball and a safe haven from the mean streets of Springfield. Coach J knew there was more to life than just basketball, however he always took his education seriously. He tried to instill that in all of us daily.

Meanwhile we returned to the courts and this exciting game that had become an offensive explosion. With a few three-point attempts and us closing the game out with free throws, the final score ended 91 to 80.

See, this was a basketball game, which you just didn't want to miss and had to be there to capture the excitement. If you missed it, then you possibly missed one of the best game performances of the year. Basketball games in the city of Springfield were always fun, and one of the top things to do, and I had made sure that Thursdays would become a day that people that enjoyed basketball would mark on their calendar throughout this season. I went on to average 35 points a game and we went undefeated to cap off another successful season.

While at the 8th grade graduation I was sitting in my white chair with a big knot in my stomach. A bright light beam of excitement shot through my quivering body. Today was the day I had been looking forward to almost all year. The day I was finally graduating from the middle school, the place that I was forced to survive for two tedious years of my life.

I was getting out and moving on. My classmate and valedictorian from my 8th grade class started giving a speech. I listened very intently. After some time passed, it was finally time for us to get our certificates. A student jumped out of the seat at the sound of his name and walked over to get his diploma. As the other students shuffled out of their seats, there was clapping and cheering as loud as fireworks.

Nervousness filled me like water being poured into a jar. What would happen when I went up to get my diploma? I was afraid of saying something humiliating and I was the top athlete as well as one of the most popular students. After waiting for what seemed like years, I got up at the sound of my name. I ran and got my diploma with, gratefully, no problems. I smiled as I heard loud whistling, clapping, and cheering all around me from my family and friends. I happily rushed back to my seat.

Afterwards, I waited long boring hours in my seat in the extremely hot weather wishing the ceremony was already over. As my mind wandered off all I could think about was going to play basketball, because I had been cleared to attend the senior high school in the fall and I had to be ready. Finally, the ceremony ended. I got out of my chair glad not to be sitting down any longer. I looked around for my family. We went to have dinner at a nearby restaurant.

From the completion of my 8th grade basketball season to the end of that summer, my stock rose because of the Magic Johnson Basketball Camp. I was an 8th grade basketball player that was from a small urban community so I went under the radar as one of the state's best players.

That was until I attended this basketball camp at Michigan State, hosted by none other Ervin "Magic" Johnson himself. See my Uncle Hollywood knew him personally and got me into his two-week camp. During this camp I got to go head-to-head with the state's elite 8th and 9th graders, and doing so I burst onto the scene going into my freshman year. With Carmen by my side I was ready for high school and whatever was to be next. High school here I come…

Chapter 3

The Unforgettable Years

Prior to my freshmen year, I was selected with several neighborhood friends to attend a leadership camp that summer. However my "real" friends were doing what they wanted to do that summer, needless to say I was not a happy camper.

Again my mother forced me without having any regard to what my plans might have been for that summer to participate in what I thought would be a waste of my time.

Who wants to go to a damn summer camp anyway? She probably didn't even ask Pops what he thought before springing that bullshit on me. He would have known that I was more interested in playing basketball and "chasing" the ladies.

My summer camp experience provided the opportunity for me to be on my own, away from my parent's dictatorship and their rules and regulations. I could now make my own decisions. So I decided since I must be at camp I'd see what summer camp had to offer. They probably wanted me to become a better leader; then there was the opportunity to have sex with a young lady that I had admired for the previous two years. I knew she was a virgin and I wanted to be her first lover.

When I found out that she was making the trip, all of my anxieties and frustrations dissipated. This was my opportunity to get to know Roslyn better. We began to spend a lot of "quality time" together.

There were many things we discussed, like guys that were trying to "hit" on her, my prior interest in being with her, things that prohibited her from dating me, her admission of wanting to be physically involved with me, how she masturbated all the time in the morning, after school and at night; she had even locked herself in a girls bathroom to pleasure herself one time and talked about how she had become obsessed with cumming. She said, "It just felt so good." Finally, she talked about how she would read a nasty story, get all wet, and then lie on her bed on her stomach on her bed, and hump her right hand.

I was listening to her, but to me something was missing. Then she said his name—DICK.

After that conversation, I began to test her just to see how horny she really was. From that day forward I would always do things to make her get wet. During the meet-and-greet dance that first weekend, for instance, I would grind on her as we danced on some of the hottest songs. I wanted to make sure she felt my big dick.

Then it finally happened a week later after the bonfire on the sandy beaches. I slipped on the girl's side of the campgrounds and she sent her roommates away...you have to read the letter to find out the details.

Dear Cherish,

After a couple days of sitting on the beach and checking everyone out through my Guess sunglasses, I saw a few really hot guys but only one really caught my attention. His name was Kendrick. Well, it didn't take long for us to get to know each other better cause we enjoyed talking to one another a lot. It didn't take long for us to get together and work things out. One evening after the bonfire, he came to my tent and I had told them lame roommates of mine to get lost.

So when he came in I had already taken my shower and put on my P.J.'s like I was going to bed I told everybody I had a slight headache. Ken came quietly in to tent and just stood there I could hear him breathing just taking shallow breaths. And in a low voice he told me how beautiful I looked and smelled. He came up close to me as we started slowly. He carefully undid my P.J.'s top, and touched my boobs... we kissed gently and pulled at each other. I got hotter than I ever have with a guy and began to feel my pussy get wet and tense. I moved closer to him, unlaced his trunks and let them fall to the floor then I saw my first real penis. And WOW!!! Oh my god it was beautiful, it sprung up to meet me. I really couldn't believe how big and hard it was.

I am used to sticking my finger in my pussy... and not even that, I usually just play with my clit until I cum. So, needless to say, I was a little worried. Kendrick was really sweet, he sucked me all over my breasts, my neck, my stomach, and my clit... his lips made me so hot and horny. I touched his dick and wanted to suck it, but realized I was a virgin and really just wanted it in my pussy, I mean I can give head whenever but first things first. Kendrick sat on the bed and I tried to lower myself onto his dick, but it was so big...

I could get it half way in, but it hurt, and I wanted him to be able to really fuck me... I wanted to feel his weight on me. We rotated and he mounted me, at first he just placed his hard dick near my pussy and made me move my hips searching for it... then he slowly pressed it into me. It was so warm and hard I really felt the best connection with him. It hurt like hell, but then again I was being fucked so I can't really complain. After about 8 strokes of him entering my vagina, we really got into a rhythm. I stopped having to cringe with pain and began to pant; he was making me so hot. Kendrick pumped my pussy and I began to yell, "Fuck me, fuck me, fuck my wet pussy...yeah fuck me." I don't even know where it came from... But yelling makes it so much better. He did fuck me, and while I have nothing to compare it to, it was so much better than fingering myself. As his dick slid in and out of me and my pussy got tighter around it, his dick got bigger and exploded so much cum into me...The best thing was, he kept pumping a little, as if he was trying to really jam the cum in me...It was the best feeling in the world. I cannot wait to be fucked again!!!!!!

PS: Hey Cherish...we're about to have bed check. I'll tell you more later!

This was the letter that was sent to Cherish from Roslyn, the chick I was fucking while we were at camp. A couple of days later I called Carman who I had been dating for about five months. I told her how I wasn't feeling camp and would rather be home with her. Then she dropped the bomb on me. She started telling me about this letter that was sent to her friend Cherish from Roslyn.

It turns out that Cherish was a good friend of my girl Carman...wow, this shit was crazy! Now that Carman had found out about Roslyn and me, she broke up with me.

Afterwards I decided to just chill and finish the camp and get back home and try to get my girl back. It was very tempting to continue sleeping with Roslyn, however, I knew that Carman might find out that we were still messing around so I just fell back.

A few days later I was at the basketball court in 90 degree weather working on my game when this sexy ass older female that was on the camp bus with me came walking on the court with biker shorts and a tank-top. She blew my mind. Her name was Lena Knight. I remembered her from our youth, and it had been a minute since I last saw her. I continued shooting and wondered to myself if she remembered me.

The court started to get packed and the guys wanted to run full court. They started picking teams and of course I got picked first.

Once the game started, I began doing me; I was ballin. The chemistry began to build between Lena and me. She was a baller as well. This chick could actually hoop and I think this intensified our attraction for one another. After we played a few games of pick-up the crowd wanted to see me and her play one-on-one. I laughed and said, "I don't play females." Then she did it when she said the magic words.

"What, are you scared I can beat you?" I got pissed because the one thing that I hated more than the "B" word was that someone called me scared, so I took her up on her offer.

The first one to score 11 points would be declared the winner. The rules were "Make-it, take-it". The gentlemanly thing to do was to give her the ball first, plus I knew the game was over once I got the rock. This chick was "thick", built like a "brick house" and she had a "phat" ass.

And she made every attempt to use that to her advantage. I had the height and speed advantage, so when she backed me down I waited until she tried to shoot then I blocked her shot. Yes, I sure did. What, y'all thought I was going to let her score on me? Y'all got to be crazy. I did enjoy her throwing her ass on me as she tried to post me up though. I ignored my being horny. I had been called out by a girl. Although I beat her, she did manage to score two points. During this very competitive game neither one of us could ignore the strong attraction that we had for one another.

Later on that evening after dinner, she came over to me and said "good game you can really ball." I said, "Thanks and so can you, you are ten times better than most of the females I've seen play. We continued to have small talk and I walked her back to the female side of the camp. Within a few days Lena and I were really starting to feel each other. Lena and I begin to establish a relationship that would continue into the school year. It was now getting close to the summer camp experience ending and we were preparing the final night activities, which was called the Steak Fry Night. Also that night, awards were given for the best overall camper, girl or boy, the best in art, music, and drama. Of course we know who received the best sportsman award, yours truly aka K-mac.

On that final day we all got back on the yellow cheese and headed back home. I then thought to myself, well the summer camp thing wasn't too bad after all. Up to this point of my life, I had really been interested in sports, although I did have other girlfriends before meeting Lena.

However, after going steady with her for the rest of that summer I noticed I had a habit of calling her and we would have long conversations on the phone.

All I seemed to think about was having sex with her. Lena was 18 and good with math. One evening when my parents were away she came to my house to help me do some "math problems." I didn't want to go to high school and not be strong in math.

As she was sitting on the bed, she spotted a soft porn magazine of my father's that I had grabbed from his stash. "Do you enjoy looking at these nasty women?" she asked.

I was shy about it, but had to admit that I did, whereupon she asked if she could watch me do it. I was surprised that she asked me that, but I pulled my dick out, lay on the bed, and started stroking it. She watched with interest and was soon to see wads of cum spurting from my shit like a water gun.

She carefully cleaned me up with some tissues and asked if she could touch my now sagging dick. I had never been with a girl four years older than me before and the excitement was incredible. She started to stroke me as I had done before, and within a couple of minutes I was spurting more come all over my belly.

Once again she obliged with the tissues and asked if I would like to touch her. How could I refuse? She pulled her short skirt up to her waist and opened her legs, exposing her white panties and very juicy pussy.

She put my hand on her pussy. I was surprised because she was very wet and I thought she had pissed on herself. She was obviously enjoying it with the noises she was making.

After a few minutes she asked me if I wanted to do it. She removed her panties and lay on the bed with her legs wide open. She told me to climb on top and do what I do.

Getting on top was easy, but now on top I couldn't find her pussy with my dick because of all of the hair she had down there.

After considerable squirming and help from her hand, I was inside her. The feeling was exquisite and I couldn't help but thrust away quickly. I came again within seconds of entering her. All I wanted to do now was sleep, but she undid her blouse and lifted her tits from out of her bra and put my hands on them.

Till then I had been shrinking inside her but now things were starting to happen again. My dick was hard again and I started to slowly move inside her.

This time I took things a bit more slowly and probably managed to fuck her for about 25 minutes before coming again. It was only after she had left that I realized that she was damn near a grown woman and she definitely was experienced far passed where I was at that time, but I still put it down because she made me her boyfriend.

Entering high school is the beginning of a whole new learning experience. Transitioning from middle school to high school presented more classes, more students, and a bigger campus. It brought new expectations and responsibilities to each of us. High school offered fresh chances to make new friends, try new sports and activities, and really explore who we are as individuals.

My goal was to maintain good grades, score high on the SAT and ACT test, and keep a positive attitude so colleges and universities would be willing to accept me.

Of course it's not as easy as it sounds, I thought it was achievable. It required a lot of work and dedication to every subject. Some of my friends breezed their way through while I was one who lived in misery trying to pass my classes. High school was a very emotional time for me, both good and bad.

It all started in 1992, at Springfield City High School. I can remember my first day of school I was nervous as hell walking to school with my friends and some other neighborhood kids, after walking four-and-a-half blocks we finally made it to the school and I was like, "Damn the summer is really over and school was about to start." Walking through the front door was unlike any school I ever entered. There were hundreds of students, big hallways, rooms, stairs and three floors. Dog, this is a large school.

An announcement blasted over the loud speaker stating, "All students that haven't registered for school have to report to the cafeteria." I started heading in the direction all the other students were going to reach the cafeteria.

On the way I ran into one of my older cousin Nancy. She was in the same grade as Lena. She was a senior and she pointed me in the direction I needed to go I thanked her and headed the way she pointed. When I got to the cafeteria area I remembered it from playing basketball games in elementary and junior high school games here at the legendary E.L.K. Bolt Gymnasium.

I walked into the cafeteria and saw all those people in there. I was like dog it's a lot of people in here, and believe it or not I was a very shy person so I quickly grabbed a seat.

Suddenly I heard a voice from behind me call my name "Kendrick! Kendrick!" I looked back and it was my best friend Orlando and a few other freshman classmates in the back of the room. I moved to the back with them. Orlando was like,

"Where did you go after we walked in the school?" I responded "I had to go to the bathroom, when I came out y'all niggas have jetted on me!"

The Principal walked in and introduced himself. "My name is Mr. Matthew Wilson." It was cool because I already knew who he was and he knew me.

I was a really good athlete so a lot of people at the school already knew of me, plus my mother had worked in the same district for years. He then said, "All the students that haven't received schedules, report to these four tables in the front of the cafeteria. They are labeled with your class year on them and there are four tables for every grade level, "he said.

After getting my schedule and locker number and combination, I headed to my locker. Meanwhile Orlando was like, "Yo K-mac, what's your locker number?" I laughed…see me and Orlando always associated our locker numbers to professional football and basketball players he said, "My locker number is 234 so that means I'm Bo Jackson." He answered,

"Well mine is 158." "So you're Derrick Thomas." I said, "Oh yeah, nigga you still remember that shit we use to do since elementary school." he said.

"Yeah, I know so don't stop because we're in high school punk!" "You right, ain't shit going to change. But little did we know everything was about to change for the both of us and very fast at that.

While standing at my locker the same people from the junior high school were still my locker mates, to my left was this nerdy chick Allegra and this cat named Floyd was to my right. See Floyd was cool because we were friends and that was ok.

Well everything didn't change because I'm still stuck with the same bunch that I lockered with for two years of junior high. I guess the change was that all the other freshman lockers were on the second floor and we were the only freshman with ours on the first floor with the senior class, they were at the far end of the hall but they still were on the first floor.

Day two, I was walking through the hall when someone grabbed my head and I was like "What the fuck?" and it was one of my older homeboys.

He was a sophomore named Nicholas that I played little league sports with. We were always the smallest players on the teams we played on but Nick had grown. He was now about 6'1" and I looked up at him now because I was like 5'6", I was like, "Damn Nick when you get that tall?" He said, "Over the summer I had a growth spurt." It was good seeing someone older that you knew but I wasn't ready for him to be so much taller than me. I guess everything had changed.

In the state of Michigan high school sports are big, so I went out for the football team and this was the first time that the coaches didn't ask me if I was playing football this year. Man I hate high school already and it's only been three weeks. Teachers and administrators don't know the half of how they may affect a kid's life.

The first real day of practice with equipment Coach Graves asked, "What position did everybody want to play" I said "I play QB, that's quarterback," and he called two other guys that played for him on last year's team that I knew I was much better than they were so he sent me with the wide receivers and said, "You can play that!" Me being me, I wanted to say fuck this shit and leave the field, but I decided to outwork and outshine.

All of the niggas over here and if I did that he'd see I was worthy of playing QB and if he didn't it would be his loss.

The first game was an away game at Baxter High. It was a Thursday night junior varsity game, upon our arrival I was a little nervous but felt ready.

The game started and we're kicking off to them I was on the first defensive team so it's almost time for me to take the field for the first time as an high school athlete. It was a surreal moment but it was the moment I had being waiting on since I was a youth football star. We suffered a crushing defeat, but the legend of Kendrick Macklemore was born, or K-mac was what my friends called me.

I scored both touchdowns. One was on an 85-yard kickoff return and the other one was a 42-yard interception return for a touchdown. So the next week I got the position I wanted.

Yep you guessed it, I got the QUARTERBACKING job. I was embraced by all of the varsity players because of my efforts on and off the field. With this new popularity came the girls and lots of them too.

After two months of high school I was the probably the most well-known freshman in the building. I was getting so many girls numbers that I had to ask my parents for a teen line, yeah a teen line. That's old school like a mug. But after getting my own line I must have talked on the phone from the time I got up in the morning to the wee hours of the night.

As my celebrity grew I started getting invited to parties and even over girls cribs and they were upper class female too. Being an undercover freak I took full advantage of this opportunity and the girl count was back on and popping.

By the end of football season I had dated about 24 girls and even better yet I slept with 17 of them. In my head I was like, "Damn!" In the eyes of my friends I was THE MAN and back then being THE MAN was the top honor with young black males so I had the respect of my peers, and the approval of the varsity players.

Though I had everything going my way in the early start of my high school career, with all the attention I was receiving, Lena and my relationship was falling apart. She felt that only she could flirt and kick it with other dudes, but when upper class females started flirting with me there was a problem. The most hurtful thing that came with this breakup with me and Lena was, one day I called her several times this particular day. Her mother and sister kept saying that Lena was not home.

Later I went to the movies with a few of my classmates. I saw Lena and this adult looking nigga walking out of a different movie all hugged up and kissing and shit.

Damn, I felt like the biggest fool ever and just wanted to get out of the movie theater before any of my friends saw her, which would cause me even more embarrassment. I hurriedly exited the through the theater doors.

The next day Lena, called and asked me, "Kendrick are you trying to see me today?" and I was like, "Yeah why not, when and what time? I got to go hoop around 5:00pm." "Ok, come get me after you finish playing baby." "Yeah, Ok," I said and hung-up. Soon as we got done balling and I dropped off Ace and Mario I headed straight to Lena's crib. I hit the horn two times and she came out.

Damn this was going to be harder than I thought as she came toward the car wearing biker shorts and a white tank-top and the ass was bangin'. It was 9:00 p.m. and I had just picked up my girlfriend. We had been together for almost 3 months now. We were in my room, and she said she wanted to suck my dick. I said bet, and she started to unzip my jeans.

By now I was hard, and my dick popped out from my unzipped pants. She surprised me by instantly putting her mouth on my throbbing dick and moving her head up and down. I was also surprised how well she sucked. I knew she had fucked with older niggas, but she never popped me off before.

As she got more and more into it I could see she was very experienced. I came and she got every drop of cum. She took off her tank top and bra. I fondled her nice firm breasts and sucked her nipples.

While I was doing this, I took off her biker shorts and panties and slipped my fingers into her wet pussy. Then she spread her legs and I licked her pussy. I went back and forth from her clit and her pussy. She moaned in pure ecstasy. She tasted so good.

Before she realized it, I got up and jammed my dick inside of her. She started to moan pretty loud. Luckily, nobody had come home yet. I pumped in and out and massaged her tits as I fucked her. I came again and she practically screamed in enjoyment. After we finished I asked her, "Why you suck, my shit? Because you felt guilt about going out with your ex that old ass nigga?" She looked shocked I knew.

Then she said "Yeah, but how you know?" I responded, "It's Springfield the city is too small for that shit..."

She started trying to explain how it ain't even like that and how he took her out to apologize for how he treated her and all she could think about is how she was treating me at that time and how sorry she was and etc. I really didn't want to hear what she was saying but it was hard to let Lena go. She was a beautiful girl but I had to let this shit go before I got hurt. So I looked her in the eyes and said, "Look Lena I really do love you, but you and I know this ain't going to work.

With you and him having this past history and me trying to come in to my own and concentrate on sports and trying to get to college. The best thing for us to do is to go our separate ways."

She looked at me and a single tear rolled down her face as she hugged me and said, "Ken I love you to and always will. You're going to be a great catch for the girl that gets you." After that we got dressed and I took her home and we shared a long and passionate kiss and she got out of the car.

I did see Lena during the next few weeks but not as much because she transferred to our rival, Springfield City High. We would run into each other at different school functions.

Chapter 4

Coming Into My On

Football season came to a close and my stock was at the highest peak it could get for a freshman. Then came my favorite time of the year; winter sports yeah boy...basketball season, something I thought I was born to do was to play basketball.

I played so well the varsity basketball Coach Carpenter asked me was I ready for varsity basketball and I was now a cocky little nigga and I was like "Yeah of course, I play ball with the guys that's on the team all the time and I always hold my own, so YEAH!" he laughed and then said "You sure do have a lot of confidence for a freshman." Then I responded with, "that's because I can back all of my talk up though!" Finally he said, "Well be at the meeting next Monday after school" and then he walked off.

That Monday came and school ended, now it's time for the meeting so I told Charles one of my buddies I played junior high with I was going to the varsity meeting so and I knew he was going to want to go too, because he thought he was as good as me.

He and I headed into the auxiliary gym where the meeting was held. This one cat comes right over to us and sat by me and asks me, "What are y'all doing in this varsity meeting?"

I was like, "Coach Carpenter asked me to come" he said, "Well what he didn't tell you, was if you get cut or don't make the team then you can't play on no other level." So I got up and went to the freshman meeting because I respected and looked up to this dude like that.

After two weeks of tryouts the teams were selected. It was December 16, 1992 and it was time for my first high school game. I was very sick with the flu and I wasn't going to play but right before my team left the locker room I was like I'm going to try to play. I can remember it like it was yesterday I took the court for the first set of warm ups and I saw my three uncles in the stands, Herman, Andrew, and Randy.

They were there to see my first high school game because my father was in Wisconsin working and couldn't be in attendance.

We went back to the locker room and I threw up all over the floor and Coach Littleton was like K-mac your out, I'm starting Charles and then they exited the room and a few minute after that they played the national anthem and called out the starting line ups.

They called my name instead of Charles's name so I quickly took the court. It was a very close game coming down to the end. I just took over in the last two minutes of the game scoring the last 18 points of the game pushing us to a narrow victory over Silver Oaks 96-95. I finished the contest with 48 points, 13 rebounds, and 12 assists my first career triple double in high school.

That was one night in my life that I will never forget. On top of that incredible game we're in a small group of girls and guys. That night I had so many girls approaching me. I was still in the middle of the crowd of people when this chick came right between everybody and grabbed my hand so I walked with her away from the group into the light and to my surprise it was my elementary girlfriend. I had not seen her since seventh grade, but damn she sure wasn't looking anything like that 7th grader that I remembered kicking it with, she was now a chocolate, teenage hottie.

Melissa and I had a history and we're only fourteen. She was very bold and was known for doing everything she just did. Well anyways she told me she was going to call me tonight so be waiting on it. I laughed…But just like clockwork she called as soon as I was walking in the house.

We talked for the remainder of the night where she reminded me she was back and, I was her man again, just like when were in elementary and junior high!' I laughed and said, "Girl you crazy." After all that I now had a girl again it was funny because I was a hot item and every girl at the school was on the new cocky freshman. We finished the year as girlfriend and boyfriend. My teammates went 19-1 but I only played four freshman games where I averaged 32 points a game and 13 assist. With those numbers I got moved to the varsity team were I was the seventh man off the bench most of the time. After getting moved up to varsity my parents had a long talk with me about continuing to keep my grades and housework up to par.

My mother would say, "Basketball is wonderful, son and I'm sure glad you're playing sports instead of running the streets, but education is always the most important thing in your life so make sure you put school before ball!"

She wouldn't let it go at that though, because I figure she'd listened to people talk about how hard it was to make it in the PRO sports.

That's why she would always end with education is always first because without it you won't have nothing to fall back on so make sure you're taking care of those books. That's what leads me to know she had been talking to people about how hard it was making the pros. And I knew that too. But I also knew that even if I didn't make it all the way, I could put some college behind myself.

And also go on to make a great life for myself. Everybody in the city who played any real ball knew my game was sweet! The team had made it to the Semi Finals the year before, and now, adding me the top freshman in the state, I knew we had a good chance to make it back down state to the high school boys' championship game.

Last year they came so close to winning but just came up a little short. But with so many upper classmen returning and the addition of me this will make for a very strong bench. The word was that there were a lot of scouts checking Xavier out at the end of last year and over the summer so I knew they would be there in the regular year as well. They always came to town around tournament time when the deals got serious.

All the older players that were on my team told me to step my game up during March, because these scouts be knowing everything from your games to your shoe size, and they would ask you questions like, "Are you involved with drugs or gangs" and "How were your grades?" because that's when the scouts would send in their reports.

The older players were telling me that the main thing is to make it back to the semis because that's when the college coaches would be making their final reports.

My high school basketball career had really just started and I knew I needed to put together three more years of the same thing to finish my career strong to be looked at by the big-time division 1 schools.

If I could get a big time deal or get picked up by a high profile program, I knew I could make it to the NBA. It was a dream, but it was a dream that I believe I could back up. Lots of cats talked the talk and a few could even walk the walk, but I knew I was out cold because I had big time skills and I was a true student of the game. All I needed to do was to live up to my ability.

The first game of the tournament was against Riverwood High. This school was a trip because the whole team was made up of black dudes and a few Latinos who could play pretty good. If they got you in a half-court game, it was over before it started, because they were a disciplined team who shot the three balls well. The only way to stop them was to run and get out to a lead and then control the boards so they couldn't get a second attempt. It also helped to beat on them a little bit if the refs let us get away with it. We went downtown to their raggedy-ass gym, checked out their fly ass girls, and had just started our warm-ups when the coach came over and told us who was starting. My coach had put the starting line up together.

Though I wasn't a starter I did play a little, but you got to remember I was a freshman on a top ranked team, so just making the team for most was an honor.

"Kareem, Malik, Desmond, Xavier, and Big Cedric are the starters tonight," is what my coach said. I think this is the best combination of players to get us the victory, "This is something I want to see if it works."

I was thinking, 'this ain't the time to see if shit works it was the first tournament game.' He went on to say "I'm still trying things out, don't worry about it." I knew the dude that was supposed to be the main player. He lived over in the Madisonville Projects on the northeast part of town. He had a funny way of holding his face, and his cousin was fine as hell, I tried to get at her a few times. She said she had a boyfriend but I end up hitting it anyway. She told me he got shot in the face when he was nine.

Everybody called him Face, but niggas didn't fuck with him because dude was a little off. Riverwood High got the ball first and my coach called for a one-two-two-zone, which is a seriously wack defense against this team. While we're falling back into a zone position, they're going past us to the hoop.

Face brought the rock down, faked toward Malik, then flew past him and made a lay-up over Big Cedric. They scored the first deuce. On defense a little dark-skinned guard took the ball away from Kareem before he got to half court. Damn, they had four points. Just about the whole first quarter was in favor of Riverwood.

They were doing anything they wanted and we were flat footed. Kareem couldn't play defense at all and was doing his best impression of his defensive move, as he watched guys go right past him. Meanwhile, I was checking out Cedric. What I saw was that he knew how to use his body, blocking out an offense and being kind of strong on defense. But he never got off the floor. It's okay to block out, but you have to jump or guys will go over you, especially if they're quick enough.

On offense he had a few moves and was strong enough to the basket, but he wasn't getting up. Twice his man slapped his shot away, and once when Cedric made a weak fake and tried an easy shot from under the hoop, the defensive guy jumped up and grabbed the ball in midair. When he did that all the girls from Riverwood started cracking up on the sidelines.

Coach Carpenter kept calling the same two plays over and over, Kareem and Malik were bringing the ball up court slow, passing in to Cedric or Rodney at the high post, then slanting across looking for the soft pick high while Xavier set up deep and rolled away from the ball looking for the inside pass, this play was called "Exchange." When we weren't doing that, we were bringing Cedric way out to set a high pick, crossing the off guard out near the top of the key, and trying to setup a backdoor, and the was shooting guard.

Either way I could see that Coach Carpenter was setting up the game so Xavier would look good, and it was all good because Xavier was an All-State and the best player, so the team wasn't tripping. The guys on Riverwood saw what was going on but just couldn't do anything about it. Xavier was just too good and they had no answer, not even from Face, he couldn't check Xavier either. As we got to the end of the first quarter, it was Riverwood 14 and us at 27. Our guys were having fun doing whatever they wanted to on the court. The second quarter wasn't the same way.

It was like practice or something, so I knew in the fourth I'd probably see some action.

Near the end of the half Riverwood hit a couple of threes and we were nonchalant the whole time. But the ass-kicking we were putting on them I'd be nonchalantly too. Coach Carpenter said, "Ya'll can't act like the game is over and just too good because there is a whole half of basketball left and we could still lose."

One thing he was right about was you never could count a good team out because Face got into a switch with Cedric because they ran a pick and roll. He faked the jumper and crossed over and headed to the hoop and threw it down all on his head and the crowd went crazy.

But on the next play Kareem passed Xavier the rock on the inbound and stopped to wait for it back, but he started down court. I was at the edge of my seat because I knew Xavier wasn't going to take that shit Face had just done too lightly.

Anyways as he was coming down court and he faked to the left, came back right hard, dipping under Face's shoulder. I knew he had the step on him as he went hard down the right base line, and then he went up and across the lane and threw it down from the other side.

It was sweet and everybody in the gym knew it and they went crazy again as Xavier hung on the rim and said to Face, "Got your ass, this is my house boy!" The ref blew the whistle and said something to both players and called a technical file against Xavier for taunting. At the end of the half it was Riverwood 28, and Knights 59. The second half was much like the first we dominated. The final score was 89-42. I did get in and scored seven of the 89 in the last two minutes of the game.

All the old guys came over to where I was sitting and told me what a good game I played in the two minutes I played, and had to keep it up, I'd get to play more, and it was encouraging to hear but I was unhappy about the minutes I got.

For real I was pissed because I knew I was better than just playing in garbage but couldn't show it because we had just won a tournament game. This some bullshit is what I thought in my head. But it's cool because every chance I get I'm going to show what I got.

That Monday morning in English I sat next to Charday Lewis, a thin brown-skinned chick with eyes the same color as her skin and spoke in a low, kind of sexy voice. We got into another discussion about Othello and I noticed that a lot of the students were saying it was about race. I still wasn't going for it.

"Iago didn't like the brother being a big time general and he didn't like him getting over with a big time white chick either," I said.

"And since he was white like everybody else around the time he has the power to mess with an Othello."

"Is it really the woman? Or is celebrity status that Othello achieved?" Mr. Morton asked.

"How do you know that Iago hoped for high office."

"I don't know," I said. "And doesn't that make the play interesting? So what's the answer?"

"Well since Shakespeare isn't around to answer a question it depends on our interpretations doesn't it?" Mr. Morton said. I didn't exactly understand what he meant by that but I could tell he was happy with it.

I see myself as Othello, a kick ass general who had climbed to the top, and had to deal with Iago and all the other suckers around him hating.

Desdemona, his old lady, was like a symbol of what he had achieved in his life and Iago was messing with it. He was saying that Desdemona wasn't really happening for him; that his dream of her was messed up. I could see how that could turn a brother's head inside out because sometimes being on the varsity make me feel the same way.

In our next tournament game against Hank Aaron Academy and Coach Carpenter ran down the lame shit about how this game was going to show our character or what not. He said that we should be able to beat Hank Aaron Academy if we played our games. Hank Aaron Academy was one of the schools that never had a real big time basketball program.

But they always had enough to get the job done and if you showed any weakness they would control the tempo and put it to you. And every year some team went over to the suburbs thinking they were going to have a cakewalk over at 134th street and would only come away with a loss.

HAA played a two-one-two to shallow zone defense most of the time. Their guards played close to the 3 point line their center played about two feet closer to the basket than most, and their forwards are in tight, too.

They cut off penetration but gave up a lot of 3 pointers coach Carpenter had Kareem and Malik, the guards, Big Cedric at center and Xavier and Rodney at forward. I thought that was lame from the get-go because Kareem should have earned his starting position not just had it handed to him.

He hadn't dominated anybody in game 1 he had played plus he wasn't kicking anybody's butt at practice either. HAA was up for the game especially on defense but their offense was weak and the game begins for me. We were up by five after a few minutes and I thought it was going to be easy but they hung on then with the slow pace they caught up and it was back and forth at the end of the first quarter it was 15 to 15.

On offense we were trying to pick off their forwards and set up back door plays but they were playing too tight to get that going. We were running into ourselves and just turning the ball over on the inside plus Malik had two fouls already. I think HAA they were going to lose before the game, but when they saw they were playing us, even they began to pick up the pace.

If a team is revving up the tempo you have to react quickly or they might get a momentum thing going on and you can't catch them. HAA ran too fast breaks in a row at the start of the second quarter. Big Cedric held the ball too low and their guard came back and slapped it loose.

The next time we came down, I saw their guards edging away from their zones, looking for another fast break. Floyd was in for Kareem and called for the two-swing play. That's when both guards moved to the right, the center comes out, and the right forward goes backdoor. The guard with the ball passes out to the center, who passes in to the forward, who is free because the other forward doesn't work, then the forward comes out and right side of the zone is overloaded.

Floyd was going to pass out to Malik but got tied up and passed it to me, and I was free. The HAA forward lost his man and picked his own teammate looking for him, which left the lane open. I went hard, and nobody even came near me as I went for the deuce.

The same dude on HAA who had lost his man took the ball out and made a weak pass that was supposed to go over my head at the foul line. I grabbed it and went right back inside, got the deuce, and the foul. Then I nailed the free throw. HAA came down again their shooting guard threw up something that looked like a half ass alley-oop, and Malik got it and flung that sucker down court Xavier was down with me on a two-against-one.

Their center wasn't tall but he was quick. I had the ball at the foul line as Xavier slid away toward the basket. I thought their center might switch when I faked the hand-off to Xavier. He did and came after me as I started to shot that was really a pass. All I saw was this big palm over my head. I saw X-man rise in the sky like a plane and catch the ball out of mid-air and throw it down with two hands, the fans went wild as always when Xavier got a crazy dunk.

We were up by four and ALA called a quick time-out. After the time-out we pulled off to 13-point lead, and held that through the whole second half. Coach took me out and they went on a 10-0 run and came within 3 points, at the end of the quarter. During the quarter break, the fans were yelling put K-mac back in the game.

But he never put me back in, and the only reason we when on to win this game is because on the final play of the game HAA ran this double screen on the baseline and there scooter caught the ball in the corner with 3 second and fire a three swish nothing but nets and the crowd was shocked.

But with all the noise nobody could hear the ref blowing his whistle. This when he said "No basket! The player was on the out of bounds line." And the gym erupted, all our fans begin cheering and teammates started hugging and jumping around.

But not the kid because I knew really we lost this game and the only reason that call was made was because of my team's record and we were number 2 in the state rankings. They wanted to see the number one versus number two in the finals.

On the bus ride home I was asked to come to the front of the bus to talk to the assistant coach named Malcolm. I declined and soon after that he came to the back and sat right next to me. "So you pissed about your playing time?" Malcolm asked.

"Yeah, I'm pissed," I said. "You think I'm not one of the best guards on this team?"

"I think the coach has the job of running the team," Malcolm said sitting next to me.

"Long as he's the coach and you're not, he tells you how to play and when for that matter."

"And so I'm supposed to be happy and go along with it right?"

"That's the way it's supposed to go, or if not then people that don't see it that way will soon be gone!" Then he turned and just looked at me.

I knew I should have said something but I just looked back at him even madder than before. Then it came out. I said it right as he was getting up, "You're a fucking dick rider." He stood up and said, "I KNOW how deep I am boy." Malcolm's voice was low, his words slow. "Do you know how deep you are son?"

I didn't really know what he meant by that, but I turned away and looked out the window as the bus pulled off. What I knew in my heart as the bus made its way to the West side freeway was that Coach Carpenter was messing with me, with who I really was as a ball player.

When I'm on the court I'm different than when I'm sitting in the class or just walking down the street. I'm the man playing ball. Carpenter knew that as well as anybody.

When I walked down the street I was ordinary, in the kind of way where I was like every other teenager around my age. I was a popular cat don't get me wrong. Never like a square or nothing, I always felt like there was a different place I was headed.

Sometimes when I hit the hood and saw cats a little older than me nodding out on the corner or standing around waiting for something to do with their lives, it made me feel real bad because something deep inside of me told me I could be heading in the same direction they were if I made the wrong choice.

All those bad feelings, that not being much, the struggle with school, all of it left me when I was playing basketball. Then the bus stopped at the school, and we took out the bags and equipment and Big Lazy and Patrick carried them inside.

I started to walk to my car, and Coach came out and said, "We need to talk tomorrow about what happened after tonight's game." I nodded and continued to my car.

The next morning I had to meet Carpenter in his office to talk about last night. He started telling me about how I had to wait my time and some other bullshit about I'm one of the "best guards on the team" but I was just too young and how I needed to learn from the upper classman to take my game to the next level.

I was thinking this nigga is crazy because I know my skills was tight I could beat damn near everybody on this fucking team outside of X-man and I'll go at him too! Then Carpenter said how he was going to add something new to each practice. The big thing in the next practice was a ball handling drill where he had us going up and down the court around cones dribbling two balls at the same time.

I didn't think much of this at first until I saw how some of the guys couldn't handle the rock as easily as I thought they should be able to. I was checking out Big Cedric, and he did alright for a big man. I kept away from Carpenter. He was making notes on his clipboard, something he had never done before. He was letting us know he was serious, but I still didn't know what he was trying to do.

We ran some wind sprints and then a wing drill. "I want the guys on defense to bring your fists up under your arms and hold out your elbows as if you had wings." Then he said "Anybody who passes you and there outside your elbows does five laps every time!"

The objective of the "wing-drill" was to go at a defender as hard as you could, but as close to his body as possible.

If you went by him close, he would have to turn his body and shift his feet before he went after you, and he wouldn't be able to do it fast enough to stop you. If you went around him too wide, he could turn his body as he moved and he could recover some of the time and get back into a good defensive position. I liked the wing drill, and I was good at it too.

Coach set up a zig-zag pattern of guys, and we had to dribble past them, always this was his attempt to ensure we played better team defense as we continued to make our playoff run. Though we were upset and lost in the next round I wasn't tripping because I had three more opportunities to get back to the Michigan High School State Boy Basketball Finals.

Chapter 5

*High School Superst*r*

The championship game was hotly contested from the onset; we were all elated and very proud of advancing to the Michigan State High School basketball championship game against our nemesis, the Marshfield Blue Jays. They narrowly defeated us earlier during the season by escaping with an 81-80 victory dropping us from the ranks of the undefeated with a record of 13-1. The Blue Jays garnered a 17-0 lead in the first quarter.

Freshman Sean Rollins scored 7 points while junior Jermey Bankhead and senior Amare Billups each scored 5 points in the amazing first half. We went 0-for-11 shooting in the first period.

During the beginning of the second period, Coach Carpenter sent me in the game to replace Malik. Immediately, I knocked down two three pointers. This blew life into our team as we went on a 10-0 run. Marshfield leads 37-29 at intermission.

As soon as we made it to the locker room our star player and team captain, Xavier McKinney, got up and said, "Come on guys we can do this. We've played these dudes tough before. This is our time to shine, so let's kick their ass and bring this title home!"

We were all clapping and patting each other on the back when Coach Carpenter stepped in and commended us all for a great second quarter but reminded us of what we needed to do.

"The game is not over yet. We have not won this yet fellas," he reminded us. "Reduce our turnovers and if we win this war on the rebounds I know we can do this. This is the time for us to stay focused, work together as a team and achieve the goals we have set for this game. Way to fight back and claw yourself into the game, but now I need everyone to focus and get on the same page. I need y'all to go all out." When Coach said this he meant he wanted us to give 110%. We all put our hands in the huddle. "One, two, three Go Knights!" We charged out of the locker room with a renewed determination.

We were tenacious, and relentless beginning the second half, we fought back to win two possessions before Marshfield went on a run of their own. Marshfield hit 10-of-15 free throws down the stretch, and controlled the backboards, limiting us to just one shot during this very critical period of the game. Three Blue Jays scored in double figures, as the other players controlled the boards. I felt that we played with heart and concerted effort during the early stages of the third quarter as we battled to get back in this championship game. Amare Billups led the Marshfield scoring with 15 points, hitting 3 treys in the game with 4 assists, 3 rebounds and 2 steals. Sean Rollins finished with 13 points, hitting a trey with 12 rebounds, a steal and an assist in the game for the Blue Jays. Jermey Bankhead added 10 points.

Our All-State superstar led us Xavier McKinney with 19 points, 8 rebounds, a steal and with 5 assist. Senior Jerome Evans finished with 11 points, 5 rebounds, and 2 steals. I chipped in 9 points on three-second half treys, 9 assist, and 7 steals, with 5 rebounds. This was a strong performance for an underclassman unfortunately, this was not our night; we were defeated by a score of 68-52, which allowed them to finish the season undefeated with a record 27-0.

As the game ended I started to get sad, seeing all of my older teammates faces filled with tears and how this might be the last time some of my teammates would get to play ball, as well as understanding how hard it is to make it back to state again. Although I was disappointed, I could not wait for the upcoming season. Lucky for me I had two more years to try and win me a state championship.

Coach Carpenter's statement to the media, "I was really proud of the way our guys played. They did everything I asked them to do." I felt like he could keep that to himself. The fact of the matter is we LOST. This was a bad year for us because we didn't win the championship, although we had some players that achieved some personal goals we came up short of our team's efforts.

Xavier McKinney finished fifth in the state for Mr. Basketball voting and made forth team All-American and first team All-State. He earned a full athletic scholarship to play Division IA ball for the Cincinnati Bear-Cats. Jerome Evans and Kareem Washington attended one of top junior colleges and became the starting guards.

Malik also verbally committed to a Division IA scholarship to play football at the University of Hawaii. I was awarded honorable mention recognition to the All-State team and was placed on the Pre-Season All-American list for the following year. I was sad about our early exit, but also excited by my own personal success.

As the season came to end we had some guys going off to college and it was looking like this was gonna be my team and I was gonna do everything in my power to lead us back to the state title game once more.

So this meant I had to work harder this upcoming summer. Now the time was upon us and I guess I was doing, too much and Melissa decided to break up with me.

One day at the run and gun, a popular community basketball summer league in Springfield, I encountered this tall light-skin young lady about 5'8" coming out of the gym with basketball attire: blue hoop shorts and a white sports bra. She was sporting short, jet-black hair that was cut low; this accentuated her beautiful face.

Her eyes were dark brown and slightly slanted with the longest eyelashes I had ever seen but what I loved most was her complexion, she was honey brown with a light golden tint that made it appear as if the sun shined at all times on her skin.

To me, she was flawless. I had not seen a young woman so beautiful in a long time. This gave her what I believed to be an exotic appearance. She really reminded me of a young version of the actress Halle Berry.

I observed as she acted out her words with the movement of her hands and body when she spoke with her friends. I was hooked the first time I saw her play basketball. She wasn't a regular girls' basketball player, she was a star in the making for up and coming freshmen with a world of talent on display, therefore a chance to make it big on the varsity level. It is not often that a talented freshman comes around two years in a row but it looked like this might be the time.

"DAMN, who is that?" I asked Cherish. She was my friend that was on the starting center on girls' varsity team. She said, "Oh that's Heather Cotton she's our new freshman point guard." I was like, "DAMN, you got to hook me up!" It was June 11, 1993 the day where I met the girl of my dreams at that time in my young life.

I would have never thought I would meet someone in high school and want to be with her the rest of my life, but it happened. One day I was at the gym shooting around and I see someone walk in as I was working out. I saw her sitting down watching me work my ass off on some ball handling drills and wind sprints. Soon as I finished my first set, I took the opportunity to go introduce myself to her. As we started talking, I remembered that my pop's and her father were good friends when they were growing up. We ended up exchanging numbers, and we ultimately became one of the city's most popular couples even at our young age.

I felt our relationship was like Omar Epps and Sanaa Lathan in Love & Basketball but before the movie came out. This girl and I were made to be with each other. After a few weeks Heather and I developed one of the great relationships. It was a platonic relationship, but it was nice.

See, this girl and I were so much alike that we could've been brother and sister, and that tight of a friendship only made our relationship better. She was the varsity girls point guard, and I was the boys', and with that we always pushed each other to get better and it was almost like an unsaid competition between us not a bad one but a good one. Whatever she did I had to top it, and she likewise.

Throughout high school, relationships are everyone's focus. More than likely the friendships between a boy and a girl will result in one type of relationship or another. While I was in high school, the types of relationships were the crazy glue relationships, the love-hate relationships, the on-again-off-again relationships, the just because relationships, the age difference relationships, the serious relationships, and friends with benefits. I experienced them all.

We were in one of those types of relationships that could be classified as a high school romance. However, all of these examples described our relationship. Two lovebirds who are always attached at the hip are participating in a crazy glue relationship is how my parents and family described us. We had such an extreme infatuation with one another.

We always felt the need to confess our love and attraction for each other often, sometimes with a five-minute long good-bye kiss before each class to feel fulfilled for the 42 minutes we were apart. For months this would be as far as we would go, passionate kisses. This was cool because Heather was a virgin, but for me, somebody that was a stone cold freak and loved sex to be abstinent, was beginning to take a toll on me. See things were all good in my relationship that was until this one day I was over my manz Doug's crib and his older sister came downstairs.

He was one of my upper-class homeboys from high school who had a sister who was older than us both. A sexy red-bone about 5'7", 158 lbs. with one of the best asses you would want to see. Her body was absolutely spectacular, not to short her beautiful face.

And I guess she had just finished working out or was about to go, because she had on her workout clothes and had a hint of sweat.

My eyes were glued to her body. I imagined I was the sweat gliding down her neck to her breasts and over each of her hard nipples. I felt my dick throbbing, pressing hard against my jean shorts.

I shook my head and came out of my daze. So as she came back down there I asked "My dude, who is that chick?"

"Who, my sister?"

"Damn that's her? I haven't seen her since we were in grade school, doc!"

"Yeah, she go to Michigan State."

"Word, she home for the whole summer?"

"Yeah, my mother got her a summer job working at her company or some shit. Damn my nigga why so many questions about my sister?? We came here to play Madden"

"Yeah, it's just I haven't seen her in years, that's all. Let's play son."

So after a few weeks I decided to ask her out on a date on the low. I think we went to a movie and went parking afterwards. We were kissing and petting through our clothes and we started opening but not removing clothes because it was cool outside.

I was fingering her wet pussy and she was rubbing my now rock-hard dick. I paused for a moment and the next thing I know she has her mouth on my dick and it is feeling great. I was so surprised that she did this, and on the first time we even kicked it. But then again she was older and had been in college for like two years and had mad experiences.

So we went out whenever we could and every time I got a great blowjob. She was 21 or 22 at the time. One night she was home from school and she invited me over. My girl was sleep and I was high and horny, so I went over there. Soon as I came over she said we could go upstairs to her bedroom. I was a little nervous because this was the first time we had actually been together at their house.

Both of her brothers were home on top of that. We stripped and she guided my head into her wet pussy. You would have had to be there to see the look on my face as my lips were on her slightly hairy pussy, it was priceless. Though we never actually had sex, I'll never forget it. I MEAN NEVER.

This was one of the first times I cheated but it wouldn't be the last as I thought to myself as I quietly went down the steps observing her brothers laid out in the big chairs knocked out from their indulgence in passing the blunt. I eased out the door with my Jordan shoes in my hand thinking, "Wow that was close!"

"Get your rusty butt up, before I pour this water on you Kendrick, you hear me!!" this was the sound of my mother's voice every morning, and it seemed like it was always when I was entering my favorite dreams. Like the one where I'm the starting point guard for my beloved Chicago Bulls, playing against their rival, the Detroit Pistons in Game Seven of the Eastern Conference Finals.

The one where I got a steal on Isaiah Thomas and took it the distance of the court and dunked on Dennis Rodman for the game winner, and my wife Halle Berry would be sitting courtside all while I'm doing it.

"You better get your butt up, boy, for the last time! It's already after seven and you aren't going to be late for school today." This was the sound of my mother's voice I would hear this for the next three years of high school.

I was always late for my first hour typing class. After a few minute of listening to my intensely inspiring pleas, Ms. Rogers, my usually unrelenting typing teacher showed me some leniency. She agreed to overlook my tardiness if I stayed after class and cleaned the classroom and chalkboard.

I quickly accepted my punishment, realizing it was a small price to pay. I took a seat in the back row of the classroom hoping I wouldn't interrupt my classmates any more than what I had already done. Once the bell finally rang, I headed to the front of the class to begin my task.

Orlando and Ace two of my "niggas" who I walk to second period biology class with were outside the door waiting while I continued to finish my task of erasing and cleaning boards. "You want us to wait for you?" "Naw" I answered without stopping making dust. "I'll catch y'all in class later just save me a seat, y'all niggas can go to second period. I turned towards Ms. Rogers just in time to see the wide grin that developed on her face. I was absolutely positive that in the three and a half months I'd been in Ms. Roger's class, this was the first time I had ever seen anything that resembled a smile.

I had always found Ms. Rogers to be extremely attractive, although her usually icy demeanor thwarted any potential crush before it developed. I had never questioned Ms. Rogers about her age but she couldn't be that much older than me, so I figured; maybe 28 or 29. Ms. Rogers had a caramel-colored complexion that I found Irresistible.

The loose-fitting clothing she wore never allowed me to confirm my suspicions, I was sure that Ms. Rogers had a banging body. The sight of the now smiling Ms. Rogers, with small dimples that I had just now discovered in both cheeks, was enough to stop my heart from beating. The crush was on, and there was nothing Ms. Rogers could ever do to make me see her as the business only educator she pretended to be. "Ms. Rogers." I called before I hit the door.

"Yes, Kendrick?"

"Can I ask you something without you getting mad at me?"

"Of course, Kendrick."

"I think you are a very beautiful woman." I declared boldly. Ms. Rogers lit up immediately. I could tell she had been caught totally off-guard by my brashness. These dimples I had wanted to see again now were much deeper than I had ever seen before.

The moment was a fleeting one, however, as Ms. Rogers quickly regained her composure. "We'll see how beautiful you think I am tomorrow if you come strolling in my classroom without your chapter review questions," she said trying to be cold again although she knew both her voice and body language betrayed her.

She was still embarrassed that she was momentarily swept off her feet by a teenage boy. See, I knew if I was grown I could have gotten her but I wasn't. But it wouldn't stop me from trying.

School was out and we were heading into the summer proceeding my sophomore year. It was really somewhat tame for me because that's when my body started going through some of its developing stages. My growth spurts were moving so fast, I was having pain in my knees on a regular basis.

Although I was young I was having the feeling of what I would hear my older relatives sometimes say that they could feel the weather change by the feeling in their bones. I was so weak sometimes I could not go out and play ball with my homeboys; I had ice packs on my knees constantly per the doctor's advice. I grew from 5'7" to 6'2", leveling off my height.

During my sophomore year, I was one of my state's top high school athletes in my class. One day I hopped in my car after a long day of practice. Its 6:00 p.m. and before I start the car up I check my pager, it was 20 missed pages.

Many of them aren't from friends or family, rather the numbers on the screen belong to college football coaches and high school recruiting "experts." The calls would continue until around midnight, and the same will happen every day, until the athlete signs on the dotted line.

They were trying to get me to verbally commit, even though I never declared which sport I was leaning towards. This is when I saw how high school athletic has become a business.

Another example of the spreading commercialism through sports; imagine being a high school athlete and waking up early for school, lifting weights and practicing afterwards, and then spending the next five hours of your day answering phone calls, pages, messages in the main office, and mail from recruiting reporters and college coaches. That is what it is like for most of the nation's top high school players.

The attention usually is welcomed, at least in the beginning. But after months of incessant interviews and questioning, it begins to get old and stressful.

Every February 2nd is designated as National Signing Day for incoming college football players, and as it approaches, the pressure put on prospective student athletes increases exponentially. This is because their decisions influence the pockets of many people.

As one of the nation's best three sport athletes I have to do it two more times, and I'm only a sophomore. I was one of those athletes recruited by over 100 Division 1-A schools, receiving over 80 scholarships.

My recruiting process began as a freshman in high school and will not end until February 2, or March 2, 1995, on national signing days when I am considering signing with the Michigan Wolverines. Michigan is my front-runner at this time because I just loved the Fab Five.

Some of my other choices were North Carolina, UCLA, Miami, and U.S.C. The process included collaboration with close friends and teammates who accepted scholarships to schools such as C, U.S.C., Wisconsin, Michigan State, Miami, and other major division 1 powerhouses some years before me.

My experience and those of other players is the main basis for my opinion along with the help of my family. One of the greatest things for me is that I still had two more years of high school sports before I really have to make a choice.

Chapter 6

Ridin' High!!!

One day I was talking to my girlfriend Heather, on the telephone. She was a beautiful virgin of 14. She had been my girl for like two years now. We had developed a strong relationship between us. She was sexy and had a nice athletic body. I liked her nice little petite ass and very long legs. I told her that I was home alone and wanted to watch a movie. I told her that I was about to come get her so get ready I'm on my way.

"Okay," she responded.

I thought that this was a chance that I could taste her pussy and fuck her. Within no time I reached her home. I rang the doorbell and she opened the door. She was looking great wearing a thin, short dress. I could hardly control myself while looking at her in that stunning sundress. When we started watching the movie I was constantly looking at her breasts that were looking nice and firm. Something about her was different today. She was staring at me, and I at her. Suddenly she stood up and stopped the movie that was on the TV. Then she popped in a XXX movie. I had not expected this one. She sat very close to me and started undressing me, taking my dick in her soft hands. The nasty scenes of the movie drove me to full emotions. I could not control myself anymore. I asked her to pull off her shirt and dress.

She hesitated but after a short time she undressed quickly and started to jack my dick. I was enjoying that moment while I started sucked her tits. She laid herself on the bed and asked me to play with her pussy. I could not wait any longer. I tried to push my penis into her pussy. She gave a loud cry with pain. She pushed me as I entered my penis into her wet pussy. She was crying,

"Ahahahahahahahahaha, oohooh, oooh, aah, aaah."

This was starting to become uncomfortable and I was ready to give up but she was not willing to stop. She was trying so hard, mainly, I think, because she was just sick of me fucking other females. She decided that she was not going to be a virgin anymore.

It was an unsuccessful attempt with me stopping because it was too painful for both of us. We stopped trying to perform the act and we just laid there holding each other closely and expressing our love that we had for one another.

I'm a student athlete entering my junior year. I'm currently in a relationship with Heather but have been dealing with eight different women during the same time. Of the eight I had slept with six of them. They were ongoing affairs. I have never once started any flirting or sexting.

These girls pretty much threw themselves at me. I knew when I started that the chicks would become attracted to me. It's common that female do. I just didn't know that it would be so many women at one time. I'm didn't think I was physically one of the finest guys in town but I know that many women did think I am handsome, and I do work really hard at keeping my body in shape.

I've been told that I have a calming, engaging personality that females are drawn to. However, I made no real effort to sleep with many of these women. I didn't romance them or date them. I rarely returned pages or calls.

Once I had one of the baby's daddy's approach me and question me about his baby's momma having my phone number. I told him straight up that I had slept with her. I know he wanted to do something but he saw the handle of my gun sticking out of the top of my pants.

The next day after practice she showed up at my crib and, yes, I fucked her again. That nigga knew the rules. If "his chick chose me" he needed to be questioning her, not me. It's all good, I let it ride. I know I will be judged but so what, I'm a cheater, fuck it. I was young and really didn't give a fuck. What these chicks were showing me was that I would be old and single.

I loved Heather but these hoes made it hard for me to trust any female. The only reason I trusted mine is because I knew she was still a virgin.

All around the country people had recently celebrated the 4th of July. It was July 24, 1994, a beautiful summer day. The weather was gorgeous but I was a little sad because it was my sweet sixteenth birthday and I had to share it with my grandmother's 60th. That day stands out because it was also when the moon blocked a portion of the sunlight and we called that the summer solstice.

Over the next several weeks, the intensity of our sexual relationship had changed significantly. We took any and every opportunity we had to continue consummating our relationship, from the car, to our families' homes, to the parks, schools you name it. We even worked out an understood arrangement with the third shift janitor to use the gym because we were both gym rats.

They called me K-mac taken from the first letters of my first and last name. I was the neutral one of the group who loved to play basketball. We had little clicks within our crew that hung together a little tighter than others. Our click consisted of Ace, Orlando, Mario, and me. Ace was the most outgoing of the crew. He and I resembled each other in physical appearance but he was very streetwise and devious. Orlando was the shortest of the group but was very tough minded.

Mario was the tallest of the bunch and had a slender frame, but Orlando was the funny man but a quiet killer on the low.

I did some things in my life with my friends, and basically did them because of my friends and mostly because of poor judgment. I can remember this one fall afternoon I was on my way to the school for practice and found Ace and Orlando doing exactly what I expected, laughing, joking, and smoking at Mario's house. "What's up with you?" Ace greeted me. "K", Orlando then acknowledged. "Fellas, I see y'all got a nice rotation going over here." "Yeah it's going be even nicer when you put your blunt in," Orlando responded.

"Oh, well it ain't going to get no better than because this one going to the face, playboy." "Whatever, you better pass that shit," Ace said. I took about five long pulls and passed the blunt to Orlando. Ace passed me the one he had.

"Ace, you hollered at your manz yet?" I asked.

"Who is that?"

"Yo manz Cyco the nigga with the work and the weed."

"The weed. Oh no doubt, I got an ounce off him earlier."

"What you need?" The blunt rotated between us again.

"I need a quack," I said, using the slang for quarter of an ounce.

"Oh naw, I don't got that," he said snickering. "I can tighten you up with a little something-something," slang for the low.

"Or I'll give you the nigga number, and you can page him your damn self." Ace said.

"So are you going seven bags for the dubb five?"

Orlando and Ace looked at each other with astonishment, and then they looked at me. "Stop playing with me, son." Ace said with a slight grin on his face. "You shouldn't even give his bitch ass the number." Orlando added his two cents. I got up from the couch and walked over to Orlando. "Man don't come over here playing and…"

His words were interrupted by the body shot I delivered. He sighed. "You going make me go get the heat." "I'll give you five for 25." Ace said. "It's a bet." I agreed. "Y'all, niggas ain't going to practice."

"Yeah soon as we get done blowing!"

"Well I'm out, Nigga. I got this Shorty meeting me before practice. She a band chick and they about to get out of band practice so I'm trying to get some third floor action before practice, you feel me?" I quickly took off and headed for the school I could see all the band people leaving and I knew she would be waiting on me upstairs at her locker.

Monica was wearing a pair of white hoop shorts. I asked her to wear them without any panties, Monica's had done what I asked her so this made me pleased. She wore an orange band t-shirt tied in a knot in the back so that her navel showed. Monica's skin, which she presently displayed to the world and the empty hallway, was a beautiful shade of light caramel.

She had wavy, sandy brown hair that reached the center of her back, and she possessed a set of brilliantly white teeth that contrasted perfectly with her skin tone.

She was down at the end of the hall with her back to me when I headed towards her she knew I was coming but wasn't paying any attention.

I didn't say a word, I just got behind her and started kissing her neck, caressing her stomach and tits with one hand while the other hand wandered down in those white shorts to tease that clit. I played with that pussy and she begin to moan softly and then pushed her ass against my hard dick.

I turned her around and kissed her with a lot of passion. I took off her top, popping those tits out and proceeded to lick and bite her large brown nipples. I was starting to drive Monica wild as she began to moan louder and mumble out "please fuck me." I positioned myself between her legs. I pulled her shorts to the side and began to thrust my dick into that warm, wet pussy.

I locked my hands around her thighs so I could go deep as possible. Trying to get deeper was turning me on more as we grunted and moaned our way to a great climax right there in the third floor hallway. The funny thing about this was I've been fucking Monica for two weeks now and it was electric, but none of my friends knew that we even talked to each other.

Keeping the secret was exciting. Then I was like, "Damn, you know what I got to get my ass to practice!" Later that evening, the whole crew was at Mario crib, there was about 15 to 20 of us smoking large amounts of marijuana and drinking everything from forty-ounce beers to Remy and Hennessy VSOP.

Everyone was high, or drunk and ready to go to this house party in the housing projects. These were some of the rowdiest and raunchiest ghetto parties around, but they were also the best. We never entered a spot before midnight because we had to make our entrance.

When we arrived we did our usual putting $2 in the pot with the winner getting the winnings of the pot for collecting the most telephone numbers. Usually Mario and I won, but I was declared the winner that night. I had gotten the names and numbers of some old acquaintances, as well as new prospects.

Amanda was one of the young ladies I met at the party in the housing projects last week. Baby was banging. She was about 5'6" and 132 pounds with the best apple bottom ass you'd ever want to see. This chick looked like she was ready for Playboy Magazine. She had the most stunning caramel complexion. Damn, she was sexy. See, Amanda like me, came from a middle class home with both parents. They lived in a good part of the city, and she had her own car.

Amanda was babysitting her younger cousin for her aunt. They had an amazing house out on the big lake. She insisted that I had to come visit. When I saw this house, I was stunned and truly impressed. You could watch the waves of the lake from the bedroom. It was just a beautiful environment. I drove out there Friday evening finding the narrow, steep driveway a little after midnight.

When I entered the place, there was no doubt that this place was laid out with hardwood floors, modern looking floor lamps, and a working wood fireplace making the whole atmosphere, I mean the works. I thought to myself as I walked through the house, this is the way I wanted to live once I got to the NBA. I followed her through this astonishing three story beach home as we walked upstairs to the second floor bedroom.

Checking on her cousin, Amanda then came back to the bedroom where she told me to sit on the edge of the bed. We exchanged a small kiss and started petting. Eventually we took turns sucking and licking each other into a frenzy, while trying not to make a sound. It was awfully exciting and satisfying.

Soon we were involved in full-on fucking while holding our breath in excitement, but we couldn't stop the soft sounds of flesh meeting or the wet smacks of penetration. I beat that pussy from the side as I drilled this 9-and-a-half inch pole into her.

Trying to be quiet was an unbearable turn-on, as she moaned, "HARDER, DEEPER YES KEN, YES KEN, I'M COMING!!!" Our orgasms were both about 10 on the Richter scale, I'm sure.

Afterwards, we lay in each other's arms gasping for air. Suddenly, a tiny cry came from the side of the bed. Then we heard a hand moving as her little three-year old cousin was trying to climb in the bed. I was shaken for a moment or two and frozen still. I quickly slid out of the bed on to the floor, naked, and grabbed a sleeping bag that was down there.

Amanda's face was full of embarrassment and disappointment as she looked over the edge of the bed at me. I could tell she wanted to go another round but it just didn't look like it was gonna happen any time soon, especially now with her little cousin in the bed wanting her attention.

Yeah, I know I talk a lot about basketball. I do want you to know I am capable of having non-basketball related fun. We'll have to talk about that on another day. Today, it's about this bowling related story. One Saturday night a group of us decided to hit up the local bowling alley.

A small gang of us entered the spot. I didn't expect to get as lucky as I did. This was just supposed to be a little get together with some good friends, but as things would happen it became a great bowling and money making night for me.

It was Mario, Ace, Orlando and myself, just to name a few. There were plenty of new chicks that had joined us and some other niggas from the hood around. We had lanes 10-12 taken and it was going down. The music was blasting, as you could hear the balls smashing the pins. The aroma of popcorn and pizza was in the air, and the girls were hanging off of the rails. We were starting to bet 10 or better and I was cleaning up big time.

Within my first few frames, I bowled three strikes, which earned me $60 dollars. This nigga should have known I was very competitive in everything I do, as I kicked it into another gear bowling strike after strike, boosting my cash count quickly over $200.

My homeboys were hyping me up, as usual, when suddenly a man from a few lanes down from our group came to our section flashing his large bankroll. He mentioned that he had been watching us most of the night, and wanted to see if we were down for some real bowling.

"Is amateur time over? Who trying to step up to the big leagues? So you on a lucky streak, huh? I think my luck is better," he said.

66

"Put your money where your mouth is," I responded.

"How much y'all betting?"

"We are betting $20 or better."

"Why don't you put your big boy pants on and let's make it $100."

"Bet," I told him.

Once the real money started getting serious, I put my gloves on and proceeded to take him on down the lane.

"Let's do this," I told him as I kept the strikes coming.

The knot had moved from his pocket to mine. The more pissed off he became, the more drinks he continued to chug down. At the end of the night, after three games, I was at my grand total of over $1,000. My crew and I finally decided to cut out for the night, but not before snatching up one of the honeys.

One of the best times besides the first time Heather and I ever had sex was definitely the time we got caught in the parking lot at the movies. We were on a date to see the movie Friday The 13th.

It was a nice long movie to get turned on by and it was full of horror. I started by holding her hand. I figured it wouldn't be good for us to do it in the movie theater itself, although I was very tempted. Instead, we went home and we fucked each other, and it was filled with passion.

Everything went as planned. We tongued each other down in the parking lot for a few minutes; we watched some of the movie. I held her hand and got turned on in the anticipation. When I drove home I asked if she wanted to have sex; she agreed. I couldn't wait until we got to my crib because I loved having sex with Heather.

Once we entered my house we started ripping off each other's clothes. I started to rub her tits; I went to rubbing her clit as hard as I could. She pushed me on the bed. I lay on my back as she got on top of me. She pushed my dick into her pussy and screamed.

After that I was rolling and stroking while she was riding my shit like a cowgirl riding a wild bronco and trying to tame it. She rode me like that for about 20 or 30 minutes until finally I shot my nut in her. I felt the pleasure subside but I knew it would come again.

We only fucked each other for like 45 minutes but I came two times in the end. Afterwards, we did some more shopping and then we went to the park. I always kept a basketball in the trunk, and since she was a player in her own right, we played a game of ball and worked on our jump shot. I can remember my junior year basketball tryouts like it was yesterday, because I felt like Coach Carpenter, again, tried to play me.

He wouldn't allow me to run home and get some hoop shorts to practice in even though I only lived 15 minutes away. Then he told me to get a pair from my girl.

"She should have some in her locker," he said. For a quick minute I did a double take not wanting to believe what my ears were hearing.

This muthafucker must've been crazy but I bit my tongue and said nothing. I quickly ran to grab her shorts after deciding, fuck it, I might as well wear these shorts even though they had Lady Knights on the back of them.

I believe this was his way of trying to keep my ego in check or embarrass and humiliate me just to control me. I figured this was yet another attempt to fuck with my head but being the headstrong young man I was I decided to play the mind game with him. The way I saw it, even if I had to wear my underwear, I could out play anybody in the gym hands down.

Soon after coming back in the gym with those tight, girls' basketball shorts on, some of my niggas and teammates began to joke me. It didn't bother me because I was about to take it to their asses anyways.

After kicking butt the first two days I got sick with the flu and couldn't complete the weeklong tryouts. On Friday morning I received a call from the Springfield Senior High School office, and soon as I answered I heard Coach Carpenter's voice on the phone.

"Hello, may I speak to Kendrick Macklemore please? This is Coach Carpenter."

"Hey Coach, this Kendrick." I said.

"Hey Macklemore, I just wanted to tell you that you've earned your spot back on the team."

I laughed in my head because this muthafucker was determined to fuck with my mind every damn time he got a chance.

"Oh thanks, Coach. I definitely appreciate it."

"I need you to get better soon first official practice is Monday."

"Ok sir, I'll be ready come Monday."

A few weeks after working and preparing hard for the season's opener, we had a pre-season game against some of the ex-players from the prior years. I played good as always. Even though Carpenter didn't start me I still did my thang. I scored like 18 points off the bench and had several highlights including a monster's baseline dunk on Matthew, a now standout football player at William and Mary University. Two days before the season opener it was time to pick jerseys. It was now my time to pick the one I wanted.

"Yeah, let me get that #22," I said.

"Naw Macklemore, you can't wear that number so pick another one. Better yet, here take #20. Don't your girlfriend wear #20? Y'all can have the same number!" Coach Carpenter asked.

As everyone in the lock room laughed, he snatched the #22 jersey and handed me the #20 jersey. I just tossed the jersey over my shoulder as he went on asking did I know who wore number #22. Now after being put on the spot, I answered with, "Yeah, Clyde Drexler, right?"

Everybody now laughed at him and I could tell he was pissed at my insightful answer but I didn't give a fuck how he felt because he tried to play me first.

"Naw, the best guard in Springfield High School wore this jersey."

I was being sarcastic, but I knew he was referring to himself. He looked at me with contempt in his eyes giving me another cold glaze.

"Ok, let's huddle. One, two, three, Knights!" Coach said as he changed the conversation.

It was a Friday afternoon, which meant game day at our high school. She was on the girls' basketball team and one of Heather's teammates but she had been flirting with me for months. Though I never fucked her I figured one day when the time was right I'll get that pussy. So she helped set up the concession stand for the boy's game.

She came into the gym to find me shooting around. I looked at her and she looked at me and we both just smiled. I looked over to see the economics teacher Mr. McCray deeply reading his newspaper.

She paid him no mind and went on to talk to me. As we continued on talking, somehow the subject of sex came up, mind you that all of the time we were together we never fucked. She suggested that we go into the locker room.

Being that I had a girl, I asked, "Why?" She shook her head in anguish as if she was mad at me, and I hated that, so I said, "Fuck it, sure." She then looked pretty surprised but wasn't completely shocked.

She took my hand and led me into the locker room to find it completely empty. I took her to the back portion, which was called the cage. I threw her against the wall and we began to kiss deeply and passionately.

Before I knew it my dick was hard in my warm up suit and she couldn't help but to drop to her knees and suck my sweet, long dick. It felt as good as she took my shit in her mouth, I wanted her to swallow it all, and before I knew it I exploded in her mouth.

She said that it tasted so great and asked me if I was surprised to see that a 16-year-old could suck so well. I then feel to my knees and pushed her onto the floor and ate that sweet little pussy vigorously.

What the fuck, this little bitch just came in my mouth. She was still wet and I was rock hard again. We fucked hard for about 30 minutes or so before us both came.

I guess all the noise we were making attracted attention cause before we knew it one of my teammates walked in. We looked up from the floor and laughed. He laughed too and said, "It's game time, Kendrick" and I said, "OK, just give me a minute." We quickly dressed and left out of different exits of the locker room.

It was the best one on one ever. No winner, no loser, just both opponents satisfied. Even after a great fuck session the first game of my junior year was crazy.

That same night, I scored 52 points off the bench and senior Mitch Butler had 50 in our three-pointer buzzer beater win 92-91 victory.

It is believed to be the fifth time two Michigan high school players had scored 50 or more points in the same game, according to Michigan High School Athletic Association sports record information, but right from the start it was anything but an ordinary game. I scored 18 points in the first quarter and finished 17-for-25 from the field, 7-for-8 from the three-point line and 11-for-12 from the free-throw line. The 52-point explosion pushed my career average to 16.4 per game and broke the school single-game record of 47 points set by George Richardson 16 years ago.

After the game the newspaper reporter came to interview me. If you would have asked me before the game if I would have thought I'd have 50+ points game, I would've said naw.

"On tonight, though, I just had it going, and my teammates kept getting me the ball once they saw I was hot. The rim felt as large as a cafeteria trash can. I just felt I couldn't miss!"

"So take us through your last shot," the reporter said.

"I just shot it as quick as I could. I thought it was gonna bounce off the front rim, but it was all net. I couldn't believe it." I said still excited.

"So what was your first thoughts when you saw it drop?" the reporter asked.

"I didn't know whether it counted or not at first, but in my eyes, it counted, so I started running around.

Everybody stormed the court. I was under the pile when we found out it might not count. Then the referees huddled, and when they said the shot was good, I started running around again and screaming. I can't believe it happened. I'm in shock right now."

Billy Westgate told me that it was gonna be on FOX Sports News Top Highlights tonight. Then he interviewed Coach Carpenter.

"So what did you thing about tonight's game?"

"It was a great game to watch, and be a part of tonight," Coach Carpenter said.

"Obviously the defense wasn't great or nobody would've scored 50."

"Yeah but with its lineup ravaged by illnesses and injuries, Edgewater High needed all of Butler's production.

The 6'0" guard had a Reggie Miller-like night making seven three-pointers. On top of knocking three down in the final 30 seconds and finished 13-for-22 from the field, 7-for-11 from the three-point line and 17-for-21 from the free throw line.

But it's a game people will always remember." Coach Carpenter said, as he walked off abruptly from the reporter ending the interview.

My girlfriend and I were driving to her home and I dared her to fuck me while we drove down the road. She was game, as she slid her pants and underwear off and moved over and sat on my dick. The motions were slow and comforting. I undid her bra and played with her firm breasts.

As I could no longer take the agony of not cumming, I pulled over and we started to grind harder.

Then I pulled the recline lever on the seat allowing me to lay down and my last two inches to enter her. She cried out, "Oh my God, Daddy!" and began to fuck harder and faster than I could ever believe. We came together in a huge orgasm. It was some of the greatest sex after the unbelievable game I had just had.

Soon after I dropped Heather off at her crib, I was thinking of Juanita who had been blowing my pager up. Shortly after I got home I called her and had her to come get me and take me to Burger King. That ride was awesome. We were caressing each other's legs while she was driving, anticipating what was to come next. We parked and she moved over to the passenger's side on top of me, and grinded herself onto me.

We kissed passionately while I pushed her shirt up and played with her breasts. She had the most exquisite breasts with beautiful brown nipples. I leaned down to suck them, holding each nipple between my teeth while my tongue flicked over them one at a time. Then I took out my dick and she bent down to suck on it. She sucked my shit like no other. She was amazing! The feel of her mouth on my dick was almost as good as her pussy on my shit. I did nut but we didn't get to fuck because she had to go pick her mother from work. To this day, I have never forgotten that night.

Over the next few games I was leading the area in points, assist, and steals while shooting 88% from the free-throw line 69% from three and having a great start to my junior season and I did all of this coming off the bench. This was the life I had the pretest girl and I was playing phenomenally things couldn't been better. I felt like a division one scholarship was in my sites and my dream could become a reality.

Chapter 7
Life Altering Experience

During the middle of the 20-game season of my junior year, things were beginning to become real difficult for me with school and my relationship with the coach. He would make comments that he felt that I was arrogant. In my opinion I was confident I knew how to play the game. There was a two-week period in which I did not play in any basketball games during that stretch. It all began with this one game in Kennedy Park, MI against the Twin Canal Cardinals.

I can remember it like the back of my hand. Shortly after the team had gotten dressed and just before tip-off, we gathered in front of the chalkboard in the locker room to finalize the key points for the playing of the game. Then it happened Coach Carpenter wrote the team objectives. They were as follows:

1.) K-mac ain't playing!!!!

2.) The offensive and defensive set was going to be... man-2-man defense and 1-4 offense tonight

3.) The top players, Terrance Reid scored 50 points against our cross-town nemesis earlier that week; we have to shut him down tonight. And we all knew Terrance Reid had just signed on to North Carolina State University that year, and Travis Green who had signed with UNLV University was there main players.

4.) Go out and play a hard game by controlling the tempo and dominating the boards.

My eyes could not move after I began reading the first line of his objectives and hearing some of the jokes of my teammates. I felt as if a ton of bricks had fallen on my chest and I was made to feel as small as wee ants we walk over every day on a common sidewalk. I felt I needed some air, so I quickly started removing my uniform and going to my locker where I had previously gotten dressed. Then Assistant Coach Malcolm dick-riding ass approached me saying, "Son, what are you doing?"

"What the fuck it look like I'm doing. Getting undressed. The mutherfucka' just said I ain't playing!" That instance when I snapped back at him, more than a million emotions were going through my head as I held back the tears. "Look…" Malcolm started to say before Coach Carpenter interrupted him with "Macklemore, take the floor or you're done!" I opened the lock-room door.

After I looked at him I grabbed my warm-up jacket and proceeded out the door. See, taking the floor for warm-ups was very difficult for me because I had to go through this whole pre-game procedure as if I was playing tonight and I knew I wasn't going to.

Throughout the game, again and again, this was still difficult. I can remember, during timeouts and breaks in the action, walking back to my seat backwards in order not to have eye contact with the crowd and trying to laugh and joke with my fellow teammates as much as possible to keep from breaking down. Instantly, my mind went back to a situation that had been ongoing with me and the coach. It began with the team being issued a team shoe order. The inserts within the shoes contained a dye that I had an allergic reaction to.

I had went to the doctor and he prescribed me some lotion and some powder to use, and advised that I only wear white socks and stay away from things that had dye in them. For this game I chose to wear a pair of Jordan's that the coach saw me in. I had presented him the note stating these instructions but he still acted as if it was an act of arrogance and defiance. I felt that his decision to remove me was unfair, without merit, and totally wrong. I knew this was the beginning of a totally different relationship with Coach Carpenter. I knew that with all my heart.

After the game it got crazier. Ultimately, we had lost and I did not care. My family of friends and supporters tried to console me but I was so emotionally damaged, I could not help myself and took my anger out on them. My dad, uncles, cousins, and Heather felt my wrath as I snapped on them all.

Since I didn't play in the game, there was no need to shower. Within five minutes I was back in my civilian clothes. I told my dad that I was not riding back on the bus with the team, and that my dad needed to give me a ride home or I was walking. When my dad told me I had to ride back with the team, I responded, "Fuck it!" and stormed off. I could hear someone behind me as I took off in the snow. When I lifted my head up and took off my hoodie I saw that it was Assistant Coach Littleton.

He was trying to stop me and explain the rules and regulations, trying to get me back on the bus. During his spiel I ended up breaking down and laying my head on his shoulder.

I needed that moment away from the crowd and have a moment to break down and experience that one-on-one support from someone, anyone, who could reassure me that everything was going to be ok. We walked back to the bus and I put my earphones on for the length of the ride. As we made it back to my hometown, one of my teammates said. "You can drop me off here I can get off here."

While this was happening I could not hear any of this but all of a sudden I noticed a looming figure shadowing over me. I turned from the window and Coach shouted, "What did you just say?" He was trying to blame me for being the one causing the drama and disorder with the team this evening.

Next thing I know we were collar-to-collar, up in one another's faces and tumbling over each other as the bus made its leans and turns getting us back to the school while my teammates instigated with oohs and aahs. As quick as it had all started, it had ended. When the bus parked, Coach ordered, "Me and you now! To the gym!" I was ready to fight him. So we headed inside, the rest of the team followed. I was getting ready to take Coach on. He challenged me with rants and comments questioning my loyalty to the team and the game.

"You don't want to wear this jersey. You don't have the heart."

I just looked at him. There were things I wanted to say but I decided not to say them at all. I even wanted to cry, but that definitely was not about to happen. As my mind was racing, there was a moment of hesitation as our eyes met.

I was thinking, this man wants me to do something, but at the same time a part of me looked at him as a grown man who might kick my ass. For a split second my rational mind was working, but I knew the best thing to do was to walk away. I ended up jumping in my car and driving off.

The next day when I opened up the newspaper, I found a front-page article on the duo, referring to them as "TNT" and their explosive 50 points they scored on our area teams. I didn't play so they actually didn't do it to me.

However, I was pissed because I was not going to have my opportunity as a junior to play against two of the best players, both seniors in the state. This would have been the kind of experience to set my destiny and put me on the map. Without that happening, all I could see was my future in basketball utterly falling apart. I never wanted to be a "he could've been" but it was looking like that was becoming my reality.

The following week started bumpy, as usual, as we came back together. We prepared to play another big game. Usually my friend, Jimmy', and I usually joke around at the start of class but today he seemed to be taking things a little too serious.

When I was messing with him this particular day, Jimmy' reacted by slapping me on the back of the head harder than necessary. I jumped up and grabbed him, which resulted in us fighting and flying over one of the desks. We both got kicked out of the classroom and sent to the office. I was then told to go see Coach Carpenter. He told me I wasn't going to be able to play the first half of the game. I reminded him of how he had sat me on the bench already.

Since he still insisted on me sitting out the game, I decided that there was no use for me going to the game at all. It was half a day at school, anyway, because of count day, which was when the district hustled to get all the kids to school to get their money from the state. I decided I was leaving the school.

I ran into one of my honeys and invited her over to my crib so we could get it on. I returned home to get some rest, and I must've slept for a couple of hours. Then all of a sudden I heard my dad come downstairs and he cut my music off. I said I wasn't going to go to the game. He said he wasn't going to play me again. I can't get picked up by a college with these points since he's not playing me.

My dad said I needed to be patient, and all that other Bullshit. I cut the music back on after shouting I still wasn't going, and my dad went back upstairs. My dad had gotten my suit and offered to take me to the game so I could still suit up but I still refused to go. My girlfriend was shocked by my behavior and started questioning me as well. I went off just wanting everyone to leave me the fuck alone. I ended up leaving and drove to the lake, listening to the Ghetto Boyz to take my mind off things.

After a few hours I went back home and was met by my dad telling me how I was wrong for my actions and not being part of the team. There was a storm that delayed the team from getting back to town that night, so when I ended up there at the school I was met by questions on why I was there and why I wasn't at the game.

The final bell had rung and we were hanging down by the cafeteria until it was time to go to practice. And this would be one of those days I'll never forget and always regret.

There were a few of my teammates and a few girls from the cheerleading team and some random folks joking and playing when Coach Carpenter came down the hall and started trying to put me on the spot. Y'all know I hate being put on blast.

"Macklemore, what you doing with that practice jersey?" he asked.

"I'm going to practice," I said.

"How you gonna come to practice and can't show up for the games?!" As he was completing his statement all I could do was look over at my girl, Heather. If looks could kill I'd be dead. I told her that I played in the game the other night, and they couldn't go because my pop's had to work, so now the cat was out of the bag. I couldn't manage to speak as he said, "You don't have the heart to be a Knight!" For me to give him my jersey again all I could do was ball it up and throw it at his face but to no avail the jersey opened up as it got to him and he just caught it.

On the low that pissed me off even more, and all I could do at that point was go to my car and leave. I went to go drink and smoke some weed. That made it official for me quitting what I loved to do play basketball. I was lost and did not know what I was going to do. I felt like I was losing my mind. I got my dad to try to get me to find Coach's house so I could talk to him and get things back on track. He wouldn't let me come back on the team and he wasn't going to let me play my senior year.

Ironically, they eventually finished the season with the same shoes I got sat on the bench for. They ended up being the team shoe for the playoffs. What a slap in the face. The team ended up getting knocked out of the season.

After the last marking period I dropped out of school. I could not be a regular student. I didn't know how to be ordinary. That was unacceptable. I was an athletic student.

In recalling being an athletic student, the activities and events are the lifeblood of that individual. K-mac reflected during this time of turmoil about baseball being cut during my 9th grade year due to economic reasons.

The football coach decided to change my position in 10th grade year to wide receiver. Therefore I was beginning to believe that all I was a single-sports athlete but now that was being taken away also.

My parents took my car and started dropping me off to school. I felt as if she was treating me as an ordinary school kid. I would walk in but go right out the back door. Eventually, I told them that I wasn't going back to school. I was sick of even pretending and walking those few blocks to go back home. I started selling drugs, knocking down chicks any and every last one I could and eventually trying to go to summer school.

All I would do was get high, drunk, get laid and gamble. I became a part of the local hood scene and was earning my street credit. People were talking about me in past tense as if I was dead, a legend, someone of the past or a "has been." Damn what a bad year this was turning out to be.

The start of my senior year was destroyed because of bad choices that I made my junior year and bad ones that I was still making at that time. Although the summer going into my senior year I did show some promise it still wasn't enough. It all started with the four summer school classes that I agreed to take.

Two were required classes I needed from the year before and the other two were to help me get ahead of most of the people entering my senior year classes. In order for me to play basketball that upcoming winter I agreed to take these summer classes this deal was made between my parents, the principal, my basketball coach and myself.

They were cool after all, plus there was this girl there that had once been my best friend my freshman year and we were attracted to each other. Actually she was a very attractive young woman. She had a beautiful dark, chocolate complexion with incredibly smooth skin. She was about 5'4" and weighed 128 pounds. She had large shapely thighs and beautiful curved hips. Renee had a perfectly round ass that remained remarkably firm, and we got a chance to flirt all summer.

She was in a relationship, and so was I, but it was something that was tempting us both and we couldn't control it. We knew it was wrong for us to be sneaking around but it was an attraction that was very real between us that we never acted on. It was because of two things: One, our relationships. Two, I had once dated her sister. Although I didn't have sex with her, I did have sex with lots of other girls that summer. It seemed like every freshman girl that attended summer school was going home with me every day. They all wanted me because of my popularity. I was the senior everybody knew.

Summer was over and school had started. I found out early that the agreement Coach Carpenter and I had made was some bullshit and he still wasn't going to let me hoop. I had just completed my evaluation with a psychologist and was still not offered an opportunity to get back on the basketball team.

So I started smoking weed and acting out big time. But this time my three-and-a-half-year relationship was even more rocky than it had been in the months prior because of all the shit that had been going on coupled with other things: me having been with all of the other girls, hanging out in the streets, the smoking and drinking. I could see me losing my girl and losing her fast.

Even though my psychologist said that I had made so much progress dealing with my anger and temper, it was a shame that this adult would go against their word.

If I would've known that he was gonna be on this bullshit I would've said fuck that psychologist shit and looked into another school, a different way to play basketball, as well as finishing high school. For a teenage, athletic, student this was damaging to me as a young man who didn't take school too serious, anyway. So with no sports there would be no college for me, because I was only an average student, nothing special, nothing exceptional. Just like everyone else.

Chapter 8
No Direction

I was 17 years old when Olivia Tucker and I were dating. She was a 16-year old, tall, light skinned, young lady. She could have been on America's Next Top Model this was before the show. She was a prototype for that. In essence, she was another girlfriend that attended our nemesis school.

However it began when she was a mere freshman in junior high school. Olivia was about 5'9" and 120 lbs. with a very nice body for a slim chick. She had a nice booty and a pair of tits to suck for hours. We had fooled around a lot, but had never done the deed because I had a girl, plus Olivia was still a virgin. She wanted to wait for marriage, and I wasn't trying to wait any longer. One night about three years after we started fooling around I got her real horny. I know I had a girlfriend, but she was the other girl that I dated in high school but not at the same building. I was anxious to stick my dick in her tight little pussy, but I held off.

We had somehow ended up on the floor in the player's palace my basement bedroom. I was sucking on her tits and kissing her all over. I asked her if she wanted me to stop. She shook her head and said, "NO". So I helped her onto the couch, knelt down in front of her, and stroked my dick until it was fully erected and then I moved closer to her wet pussy. I eased in and she stopped me.

"It hurts," she said. I told her that it would just a little but not to worry, I'd be gentle.

I pushed in again, feeling my dick stop against her inner wall. I pushed again and again, but since this was also my first time getting this pussy, I nutted after about 30 seconds.

It hurt her a lot but we kept having sex after that. It hurt her next couple of times, but then got better for her. Damn, now I was caught up between two women and I cared about them both. This was my substitute for basketball.

It was Memorial Day weekend the fall of my senior year and all of my family was in Mount Hope, Michigan for a family reunion. I'll never forget this conversation me and my Uncle Fish had that day. It all started when he asked me, "Boy are you still going to school?"

"Something like that, Unk." I said.

He gave a slight frown as if that was not the shit he wanted to hear. "Something like that, what fuck does that mean? You go when you please?!"

"Yeah Basically."

My uncle shook his head at the response. "So what grade are you in now?"

"The twelfth."

He looked all the more confused. "So you've never had to repeat a grade?"

"Nope, but I did come close last year. I had to take four summer school classes but I managed to do enough to pass."

"And what kind of grades did you get before this year?"

"I Passed!"

"No D's or F's?"

"I got a couple of incompletes when I stopped going to school at the end of my junior year, but after summer school and extra work my grades were good enough to pass. But I've dropped out now. "

"So after that you're only a few months from graduation and you wait until your senior year to give up," he said angrily. "Are you in these motherfucking streets?" he asked.

"KNEE-DEEP!" I said kind of ashamed. A few weeks ago, I was somewhat proud of being a thug, but with the burdens of the lifestyle, I wasn't feeling the shit anymore. My uncle nodded in agreement.

"Are you satisfied with the life you've been living?"

"Nope."

He nodded again. "Are you confused?"

"Yeah, I am."

"Son, I've been there but I got some advice for you. It will help you in the long run, but in the meantime it will likely offend you and cause you to have more questions. Some of the truths I'm going to tell you will be directly related to the vision our family has for you. Are you ready for me to go there?" he asked me.

"Yeah tell me what I need to hear."

"Well first of all you are a slave. Yes a slave. You are a slave to sin; you serve it well and proudly. Therefore, you are also the devil's servant."

"WHAT?!" You could now see the outrage on my face and hear it in my voice; it was clearly evident that I was offended.

81

"Just bear with me and listen. What I'm saying is that you either serve the Lord or the devil and your way of life represents the devil son. I have heard some of the things you have done; some of them were horrific. Whether you are ready to acknowledge it or not, your actions speak for themselves, you have to realize that first.

Now this is a bit complicated. The devil has in the making a centuries old plot to force World War III, the final such war of that magnitude. Though he has been laying down the groundwork for hundreds of years, he needed someone to get the ball rolling. Can you guess who that somebody is?"

"I don't have time for a lot of games right now," I responded.

"You see, that's his influence. His demons that you serve tempt you into being impatient, angry and ruthless. They are all around us right now and they want conflict. Nephew, I know. I was in The Vietnam War. And those demons feed on it and it makes them stronger. Don't believe me for a second, they are not around because you cannot see them.

They are running rampant in this city and the world. I'm sure you've heard that saying 'the greatest trick the devil ever pulled was convincing the world that he does not exist.'" I then, out of anger and frustration said, "Are you sure you ain't seeing demons because you drunk or smoked some bad weed or something?" I asked trying to offend him since he didn't seem to care about what he said to me.

"Oh, I'm good, but that's one of their powers over man. The drunk or drug usage card. See you're being attacked by demons right now. And what is your excuse? You weren't raised the way that you are acting. So what made you change so much for the worse?" In my head I was think peer pressure but what came out my mouth was, "I don't know what you're talking about."

"I bet. Like I was saying though, you aren't that person. You are the person who will press forward with your plans and dreams. The devil knows you are in the Lord's hands. That's why he chooses you for the most part, so he can throw it up in the Lord's face." My uncle paused so he could study me a moment. I was very pissed with the shit he was spewing and was ready to go so I had no reply. I just mean mugged him and walked away, he continued talking in his drunken state.

I paused for a minute looking at him as he threw back the last of his drink, and I continued to walk away in the opposite direction thinking all the time, this old dude has lost his mind. A few weeks later I was sent to live with my aunt in another state. I was excited about moving to a new city.

Because of my mother, I got forced to move to Maplewood, Indiana where I knew I had to start all over: new friends, new house, new everything. It was depressing to know that I had to leave Heather, the love of my life, and leaving my crew was hard.

I was scheduled to begin my new school at Benjamin Howard High two days after I got there. I racked my brain trying to think of a positive solution but just not coming up with anything. I decided to call my cousin and talk to him and see if he had any ideas. After an hour of talking and still not coming up with anything, an idea came from out of the blue. My cousin Jada lived in the city where I was. I thought maybe it would be a possibility to live with her instead. My mother was not too keen on that idea but we eventually decided it was the best option.

My Aunt Theresa and my mother got along well but they are two completely different people. My Aunt Theresa has more of a militant personality and did everything with military structure whereas my mother enjoyed life, very outgoing, and loved spending time at home with my father and family.

Mom made the phone call and called me back to say that everything was settled and that Jada would not mind at all. It was settled then, I packed my belongings and headed out with about one week to move in and reacquaint myself with my cousin.

Driving up to my cousin's house I wondered if I had made the wrong decision. I walked up to the door and was happily greeted by my favorite cousin Jada. After exchanging hellos we adjourned into the sitting room to catch up on each other's lives.

"So Kendrick, you're still a big shot, basketball player right?"

"Naw, I wasn't able to play at my last high school. I just wish that I had been a little more careful with my attitude. I hope I can play here." I said.

"Yeah, don't worry you can probably play on the team here. You can find out tomorrow when you get to school." Jada replied. "And don't worry I will stay out of your way and you can come and go as you please."

"Thanks, that is very kind of you, Jada, and don't worry I will stay out of your way as well," I said.

"So tell me, Kendrick, what else have you been doing since I've gotten out of college?" Jada asked, "I haven't seen you since I've graduated."

"Just working, on my basketball skills. I have been very busy with trying to make this my career and haven't had much time for anything else outside."

"Oh boy, you are a boring one, huh, Kendrick?" Jada replied. "Do you have a girlfriend you left behind?"

"Yeah, I'm still with Heather and it's been up and down but we still hanging on. It'll be four years."

"Well you have certainly grown up and matured since I'd seen you at my college graduation a few years ago." Jada said. "You have grown into a handsome young man."

"Thanks, Jada, and you look like you haven't aged a day since then." So after our two-hour conversation I headed upstairs to my new room. I picked up the phone and called Heather.

"Hello?" She answered.

"What's up, baby girl? How was your day?"

"Who is this?" she said. I got pissed off ASAP

"Who the fuck you think it is calling you baby girl? You still talking to that clown-ass nigga behind my back? So I leave and that's what you do?"

"See, there you go with that crazy stuff again! I just couldn't hear you and you just jumped to a conclusion."

"Look, I'm sorry. It's just hard being away from you and my niggas. On top of starting a new school tomorrow. It makes me a little nervous, you know."

"Yeah, baby, I know it's not easy for me either. But if you just be yourself things will work out."

"Ok your right, love you. Goodnight."

"Love you too, Kendrick. Goodnight call me tomorrow and let me know how your first day goes."

As I lay down that night, there were things on my mind the rest of the night. I knew starting at a new high school was one of the most difficult changes in my life. I couldn't help but to feel both excited and afraid about the process. See, it was hard for me to leave my old school.

You know how that is having been the cool kid and holding a reputation and the same friends all this time. Now I was starting over, and not only in a new school but a new city and state. It is what it is, you know.

In this overnight process, I looked at it like "fuck it." If it's in you, your realness will shine so I couldn't wait to move on to my new opportunity.

The next morning I woke up early and headed to the bathroom to shower. I had a million thoughts running through my head the whole shower. Here it is the big day. See, you can be really excited about this or really nervous.

Just remember that no matter what the situation is, always be yourself. I was walking down the main hall and you could tell I was the new person, and not only could you tell but it felt like they were all staring at me. So being I didn't know anyone, I tried speaking to this cat whose locker was next to mine. I could tell he was a nerd because he really appreciated me speaking to him. I asked homeboy where my first classroom was located.

"I'll show you if you don't mind me walking with you." First I looked at this nerdy mutherfucker like "Hell Naw" but then I remembered I didn't know how to get around this big-ass campus.

This school looked like a small junior college. So I said, "Yeah that's cool doc." As we walked down the long hall now more than ever before everybody was looking at me walking with this damn nerd. I knew this was gonna' be a hard transition.

After my first three classes I went to my locker and put my books up, and went off to lunch. Prior to me receiving my food, I looked for a table and they were all full with the different groups of people from the jocks and popular kids to nerds and misfits, and the only seat in the lunchroom was next to…yep, you guessed it the damn nerd.

He was more than helpful though, giving me all the information on who was who and what was what. Soon after we finished eating all the people were going into a gym. They were about to hoop. It was most of the basketball players, so this was my chance to show my stuff, but damn this would be a day when I didn't have any shorts. Fred, the nerdy dude, said he had some shorts in his gym locker and quickly went to get them as they were shooting for captains. I picked up the ball and went to the top of the key and shot. First shot I dropped it, so I was the first captain.

As they continued to shoot for the second captain I went to the bathroom and put on the shorts Fred gave me. I picked four other cats and we played. I kicked they butt. I scored like eight of the 11 points.

Little did I know but the assistant coach was watching me the whole time, but after putting on a show like I did all the niggas on the team were giving me mad props. I could see that the chicks were starting to feel me too.

During fifth period, I was called out of class by the athlete director and the head coach. They asked me where I was from and if I wanted to play ball for them. You know, I was like, "Yes sir, I would love to be a member of your team." Though I had to wait until my transcripts got there I could practice with the team. Things started to look up for me but there was something still missing. Yep, my baby Heather, and things were as rocky as they could get and I was four hours always. Then this school turned out to be a different kind of academic expectance for me.

This was the Maplewood High School in Maplewood, Indiana and their mascot was the Falcon. They took my word that I was a senior and enrolled me in courses like Math, Science, English, and History. It was different because each course had a thing call a "syllabus." What was this place—a darn junior college?

Somebody told me that the senior class of the previous year graduated 2,100 plus students last year. I was thinking at my old school we didn't have 2,100 students in the entire build. When I went into their gym it reminded me of the arena that we played our tournament games at. This place was so big that the Indiana Pacers could use it for a home game.

After about three or four weeks of going back and forth to classes, one day the athletic director (AD) called me into his office and informed me that my old school had not sent my transcripts.

In order for me to be able to play I had to get them ASAP or I would not be able to play until the second semester. Again my heart dropped. I knew if I was not going to play ball here that I might as well return to Michigan and be with my girl and crew.

Soon as I exited the building through the back door I saw some cats shooting craps and figured I'd try my luck. Fuck it, I had $10 to lose and about 30 minutes later I'd walk away $58 richer. I was walking to my cousin's house I started thinking about what the AD was talking about and how I was going to see how or if I could get Springfield High to speed up with the transcripts. Then the idea hit me that realistically I wasn't going be able to get those transcripts before Monday's deadline. So I decided to take my little dice money and buy a bus ticket home.

When Jada came in from work I asked if I could use her jeep to go to the mall, but little did she know I was going to the Greyhound bus station to get that ticket. It was nothing that Jada or Aunt Theresa had done, and as a matter of fact not even the city.

Again, I was without basketball so I figured if I wasn't going to play ball here I may as well go back home to be with my girlfriend and homeboys. After a six-hour bus ride, I was back in Springfield. I called my pop's from the pay phone and told him I was in downtown Springfield and needed a ride home.

Shortly after my return to Springfield, I met this lil' chick named Tootie. Baby had the sweetest body, creamy tan skin, a little extra meat on her bones, dark black hair, big brown eyes, a shapely ass and nice big breasts. A few days later I was at this lil' chick's house and we were talking about love and sex.

She said that she was feeling me. I had thought that about her for a long time already. She was wearing a low cut spandex shirt and a mini skirt, that's all.

No underwear. I quickly agreed and jumped onto the bed. She was young but way to advance to be a virgin I thought to myself. I started by pulling off her shirt, squeezing her nipples and licking all over her round, full tits. I could tell I was driving her crazy. I unzipped my pants and took out my thick, big, hard dick. She said, "God, you must have 10 inches?" She started stroking it and in about ten minutes I came without even touching her pussy. I groaned, "You're a sure thing, aren't you?" I slipped my huge dick into her pussy as she got on top. She rode me until I flipped her over and slammed all dick into her.

"I'm gonna fuck you better than you'll ever be fucked again, you little hoe." And I did. She had to muffle her screams with a pillow. I got her off many times that night, more than any other guy ever could, she said. I finished by, again, sucking them nice, firm tits. Then soon as I got dressed I instantly felt bad.

Not bad because I just fucked this chick, but bad because I had cheated on my girl once again. So having a guilty conscience, I called my girl and told her I was on my way over. On my way to her house I stopped at the gas station to grab a Power-aid and this cat asked me, "Yo, playboy you got chronic?"

"No doubt, son. Come to my car with me and I'll hook you up. So what you trying to get?"

"Just a quarter right now, but if its potent you my manz!"

"Fasho."

"Yo don't you play for the Knight's basketball team?" I was known throughout the city and state.

"Yeah, I'm the starting point guard for them," I responded.

"Y'all going down state this year?" he continued asking.

"Hope so. I'm gonna do my part. Alrite, doc, it's gonna be $30 for that quarter."

"My dude I got $27." I knew he had $30 but fuck it it was three dollars. As he handed me the money I gave him the bag, dapped him up and cut out. After talking to old boy, I thought to myself about how I had just lied to this nigga about still being on the team this year. I was also still feeling bad about what I had just done.

I had to do something for Heather, so when I got in the house I asked, "Baby, have you ate yet?"

"Naw, why?"

"Because I was thinking we should hit the mall and then grab some pizza."

"Ok, that's cool," she replied.

The summer after my senior year in high school, all of my friends had just graduated and were getting ready to take off to college. I was preparing myself to be left behind and figure out what I was going to do with my life as a diploma less adult. I was a real angry young man and did not have a care in the world so this made me a candidate for prison.

While I was dealing with those thoughts, one of our classmates and a very good friend was killed a week after graduation. This was the second classmate that we had lost to death and the experience wore greatly on everyone. Without a doubt this was a very difficult time for me.

My parents tried an intervention with me by suggesting that I go to The Miracles Building, and adult alternative education school to complete my education. My other option was to get a job or get my ass out of their house and take care of myself. I really wasn't ready to do any of it at this point in life.

They also offered to pay for the cost of me going to college as long as I finished high school and would go full time. I would have to start right away after completing the adult alternative program. They believed that I would be more prepared for the challenge of the real world by having a four year college degree rather than just a high school diploma. Having a higher education made the difference in getting a good job with a decent salary.

Unfortunately, I did not follow my parents' advice, I did not finish high school nor, did I go to college. Instead, I decided to look for a job because I wanted to be "independent." I had been working at different dead end jobs and making minimum wage. I tried to apply for better jobs that would pay more than just the minimum wage.

These jobs required a high school diploma, which I did not have. I soon realized that I had to go back to school to obtain my diploma or GED. Instead of that, I found myself selling weed and gambling and it was ok for the time being. There was always room for improvement, though. I hated the fact that I had basically wasted a year.

I didn't know who or where to turn for advice. This was a very tough time in my life for me, and I knew that I was a confused young man. I couldn't go to my parents because I didn't want to hear how I let them down. I couldn't go to my family because I'd get the same reaction and I'd never bother my friends with my real personal thoughts. I was trapped with these inner thoughts and feelings.

With those feelings of confusion, doubt, hurt, anger and distrust I felt transformed from a nice little small town boy plagued with demons to a man who'd acquire a bold style as I embraced the street life.

Chapter 9
"Uncle Hollywood"

I can remember it like yesterday. I was a 20-year-old single black man and I was ready for whatever the big city and bright lights had to offer a guy like myself. This was a move inspired by my favorite uncle, "Uncle Hollywood," which is what I liked to call him as a result of his suave characteristics.

He was smooth, debonair, and a slick, talking cat standing about 6'0" tall, weighing 190 pounds, with a light, skinned complexion, and wavy hair. He had a great personality with a gift of great conversation. The year was 1997. I was headed to California to start my life over. My family and I thought that this was a good move for me at this point of my life when I needed to get away from my old environment and start anew.

Uncle Hollywood was connected to the real estate movement and had the game on lock. Unk and his wife Joyce resided in a $2.5 million dollar crib that had seven bedrooms, five bathrooms, and a four, car garage in which he sported a Range Rover, BMW 747, Bentley Coupe and his wife's black Jaguar.

This is one individual that I would definitely declare that many qualities in which I possessed derived from his aura. I had moved in with Uncle Hollywood and Aunt Joyce by the end of the summer. Being so heavily connected in his field of work, he hooked me up with a job right away. Although it was not the dopiest nine to five, it was still a gig that brought in steady income.

The job was working at a golf course, where my duties were to wash and park the golf carts. It only paid $11.25 an hour. Now, this is something I can do for eight hours a day, you feel me? He hooked me up with all types of connects while I was there.

He not only had them all over the city but throughout the state as well. The first resource I had the opportunity to meet was this dude named Jeff, a light, skinned dude with a high top fade and freckles. To me, he was a Sinbad look alike. Jeff was also from Michigan, however, he was born and raised in a little city called Twelve Oaks. Uncle Hollywood and Jeff met while they both attended Michigan State University where they acquired degrees in Business Management and Urban Planning, respectively. Jeff and Unk met at Michigan State University in 1979.

Yep, the same year Magic Johnson and the Michigan State Spartans won the National Championship. Immediately following graduation, Uncle Hollywood and Jeff took their separate routes in life, Unk moving to Dallas, Texas after a short stay in Lansing, Michigan. Shortly after arriving in Dallas he began working for a big time real estate company, where he was employed for seven and a half years.

This is one person that had a lot of influence on me and made a major impact on my life. He had it all. Not only was he a fly dresser but he had mad women and had his way with them, and I don't use this term loosely. Every time he came home to visit he had a different chick and a pocket full of money. I wanted to live life just like my cool ass uncle. Living in the city for a few years, Unk had ran into his old college buddy Jeff, who was working at an Italian suit shop during that time.

The two of them had not seen each other in years so they exchanged numbers and continued to kick it from time to time when their work schedule permitted. After a seven year, long stint, Unk decided to continue to make moves, this time to California, or should I say the home of Hollywood and the place where dreams are made reality. Nevertheless, Unk, with his smooth gift of gab transitioned himself with a position at a Fortune 500 company where he received a crazy contract. I have to say Unk was doing it real big with this new move.

Little did he know that with this new job that he would get himself into more than what he bargained for; just like the saying goes, "More money, more hoes, more problems." He definitely had stepped his game up with this job though.

The promiscuous nature of Uncle Hollywood forced him to run through bad chick after bad chick, until one day as he was driving down West Hollywood he noticed probably the most beautiful chick he had ever laid eyes on. She was walking down the street standing about 5'8" or so, hazel eyes and a caramel complexion. She had the walk of a runway model, and him being whom he was had to have her.

She looked like she had just stepped out of a magazine. He pulled right up to her and said, "Sweetie, I didn't get your name?" She kept walking and shopping as if he did not exist. Damn, Unk got dissed. He quickly found a parking garage to park his black on black 500 CLK Benz.

He was now off to the streets with the intention to find this mystery woman. He searched high and low looking for her like a dog in heat seeking its prey.

After walking up and down West Hollywood, she came out of the Beverly Shopping Center with a gang of shopping bags. He spotted her and once again began his pursuit. He chased her until he caught up with her. As he approached her she dropped her keys, startled by his appearance. He quickly picked them up and returned them to the beautiful woman as she reacted with obvious aggravation, yet thanking him.

The woman proceeded to reach her destination. As she turned and started to descend away from him, he aggressively grabbed her arm and swung her around with the intention to stop her.

She angrily responded to this behavior by asking him, "WHAT DO YOU WANT FROM ME???" As this beautiful woman showed signs of frustration and disapproval by the rolling of her eyes, Unk saw no better chance to cut into this woman. The woman again replied, "Can I have my arm back, Mister?" So he let it go and extended his hand to her. Unk being the player that he was took this opportunity to introduce himself.

"My name is Morris King. I'm just trying to get your name, madam."

"You think I'm an old lady or something?"

He politely laughed and responded, "A sexy woman like you, I would have to be blind, crippled, or crazy to think that you were an old lady."

The woman smiled and said thank you. Unk knew right then he had her.

"I'm Morris and your name is?"

This time she responded with her name, Whitney Valentine.

She threw him a half smile as she noticed his eyes. They were kind of turning her on.

"Nice to meet you, Whitney."

"Same here."

"So, Miss Valentine, are you seeing or dating anyone?"

"No, I'm a single black female. Well, I'll be going now. Peace."

"So, what's the rush? You say you're single; you should have time to mingle. I just want to treat you to dinner."

This rendezvous on the streets of West Hollywood progressed from that point on as Unk and Whitney dated for about five years. Whitney had a daughter and worked for a big insurance company. She and Unk made a prefect couple and I believed it to be a match made in heaven. Every time Uncle Hollywood and Whitney would come to Michigan to visit they shined like two superstars. One fall day afternoon while Unk and Whitney were out on Rodeo Drive, a guy approached the couple yelling his name.

"Morris? Morris King is that you?"

"Jeff?" responded as both men laughed.

"Man, what are you doing here? The last time I saw you, you were selling suits in Dallas. So do you live out here now?" Morris asked.

"Yeah, I've been living here for almost two years now. I got my own suit shop now."

"Man that's great!" replied Morris.

"I apologize for being so rude. Jeff, this is my lady, Whitney. Whitney, this is my good friend from college, Jeff."

"Hey we're just down here doing some shopping and site seeing. Would you like to have lunch with us, Jeff?" Whitney asked after the introduction.

"I can't, I have to get back to the shop but here is my card. Morris, give me a call so we can catch up and stay in contact," Jeff responded.

Unfortunately, as time went on, Unk and Whitney began to grow further and further apart, ultimately ending their relationship. Unk was now single again, and at this point really unhappy with his company. Everything seemed to be heading south and something had to be done and done quickly. With all of these misfortunes that life has brought into Unk's life, he was in search of a way out. He decided to go back to school and pursue his master's degree at San Diego University. As he put this plan into motion, he met this mature, beautiful and very sexy red boned woman who he began dating. Her name was Joyce.

They quickly fell in love and got married after about three years of dating. Joyce had a 20 something year old son who lived in Northern California with his wife and kids. Even with all the new additions, Unk still managed to maintain his own personal values, focus, and self-drive, thus, venturing out and starting his own real estate company, The M. King Group, INC.

Although Uncle Hollywood and Whitney had not been dating for some time at this point, on June 8, 1997 Whitney invited two close relatives and myself to California for a two week vacation and the attendance of her 18 year old daughter's graduation.

On this trip, Candice and Brock, who at the time were 18 and 14, respectively, accompanied me. Upon arrival Whitney challenged me to a game of basketball against this high school kid who was supposed to be really good.

The guy's name was Baron Davis and he was a High School All American who was headed to play point guard at UCLA. It wasn't anything to me because when it came to hooping I thought I was the best, so we went down the street to the local park and played the first game. I won hands down, 11-3. The second game was a battle, 11-9. The last game he won, 11-6. So, I won the bet and Whitney had to get me whatever I desired.

After that, we went to a few pool parties at some celebrity houses. Aaliyah, Whitney's daughter, knew where all the celebrities lived, as well as hung out. We went to Mario Bennett's pool party. At the time he was part of the NBA Lakers. I saw all kinds of superstars, like Nick Van Exel, Eddie Jones, and the rookie, "The Kid", Kobe Bryant. Mind you, everybody wanted Kobe.

The next day we were at R&B icons KC and Jo-Jo's house, where I saw a lot of entertainers, actors, and artists. In the middle of the week we went to Aaliyah's graduation where she finished in the top 10 of her class. At the graduation I spotted this cold chick in a black fitted dress. After the graduation I asked Aaliyah did she know the girl; she said she was one of her best friends.

"Do you want to meet her?"

"Hell yeah!"

So, Aaliyah introduced us to one another. Her name was Trina.

"Trina, this is my cousin Kendrick from Michigan. He wanted to meet you."

"Why didn't you come up to me yourself?" Trina asked me.

"It's your graduation and your family was all around. I just didn't want to be rude, you feel me?" I responded.

It was like two days later and Aaliyah's boyfriend, Rick, and his friend Baron were graduating from Crenshaw High School, a nearby high school. We all were present Trina, Aaliyah, Candice, Brock, some of Aaliyah's other friends, and myself. It was a very big graduation class.

Something like 3,800 people, and it just didn't end there. One of the graduates was the first cousin of rap star Lil' Kim. Silly me, not knowing she could sing just as well as she rapped. She sang a song to salute the Crenshaw High School Class of 97'. This will be something I'll never forget. They have this big party for all the graduates of the year at the Coliseum. It is a can't miss event. We kicked it at the party until like 2:30 am until a couple of gang members got into it and they quickly turned the party out. After leaving the Coliseum a gang of people went to Denny's to eat. We ate and cracked a few jokes. Then Rick suggested we run out on the bill, so everybody ran for the door, jumped into their cars, and jetted on them mugs.

On Saturday, Baron and some of the guys that were on his future team at UCLA asked me to play in a basketball tournament that would be held outside of the old Lakers stadium. The tournament was sponsored by Nike. And then there was Trina one of Aaliyah's best friends who happened to be in the "Doin' It" video by L.L. Cool J.

She was a very attractive girl and had just done her first music video, and she was feeling your boy. After the basketball tournament we went on a date. Later that night I hooked up with Trina's badass. She was 5'7", about 138 pounds, and light skinned with a fat ass, I must add.

We did the typical date thing, dinner and a movie, but she took it a step further and took me to Venus Beach were we walked on the warm summer sand to the ocean. We were walking and playing in the water and she decided to pull me into the water on top of her. We started kissing and touching. She was grabbing on my dick like a door handle and she kept whispering,

"Take me now, daddy. Take me now."

"Damn, right here?" I asked.

She looked at me with lust in her eyes as she said, "Yeah, right here; fuck me!"

I reached in my pocket and pulled out my condom. She started licking and sucking on my hard dick and moaning, "Get this pussy, daddy!"

As she popped me off I was getting close and about to nut all over. I got up, put the condom on, and she began to ride me like a cowgirl rides a bull. Frontwards, backwards, and sideways. Then I was getting it doggie. I was beating that pussy back.

When she was about to come, she screamed out, "Deeper! Harder! Yes, that's it. Oh my God, I never had an orgasm like that before."

We winded up kicking it a few more times before I left to see my Uncle Morris in San Diego.

The next week, Candice, Brock and myself got on the train to San Diego to see Uncle Morris and Aunt Joyce. It was a very nice trip that took us through the mountains, along the ocean side, and rolling past the Anaheim Angels Stadium and Orange County. We finally arrived in San Diego, and like clockwork Unk was waiting for us when we got off the train. He greeted us with hugs as I asked him what he was driving, which he responded, "I'm driving my Range." On the drive to his house he asked us if we needed anything.

"Yes, I would like some ice cream," Candice responded.

We stopped at this plaza and stood in line to get ice cream. While standing in line, these chicks were checking a nigga out so Unk went over to them and did what he does best. He swiftly called me over to them and introduced me to the young ladies. I exchanged numbers with them and we cut out, going to Unk's crib.

Soon as we pulled into the driveway, Aunt Joyce was pulling in also. She jumped out of her car and gave everyone hugs and kisses, then we all went into their house. Joyce and Unk prepared us the best seafood dinner you would ever want to have.

They had everything from crab legs, tails, and shrimp for days. After we ate, everybody just kind of kicked back for the night. Then the phone rang.

"Kendrick, you have a phone call," Aunt Joyce shouted to me. I figured it was my mom or dad on the phone, so I quickly grabbed the phone.

"Hello?"

To my surprise it was a female voice on the other end that said, "You told me to give you a call when I got home, and now I'm at home. I decided to call. What's up with you? Or do you even remember my name?"

"Yes, I do it's Camille, right?" I responded

"Yeah, that's me."

"So, what do you know good?" I asked.

"Nothing. Bored out my mind trying to find something to get into for the night."

"Dig, that's me too, so I guess we could find something to do or just be bored together, if that's cool with you?"

"That's fine. So how long are you staying and what part of town does your Uncle stay on?"

"Like a week in a half, and I can ask him because I really don't know. I'll let him explain where he lives and how to get here, if that's ok. I'll put him on the phone, hold on."

As she held on for my uncle to get on the phone, I started to get the room together for her arrival. Meanwhile he was giving her directions to the crib.

"Yo, Unk, so what she say?" I asked after they hung up.
"She said she would be here in like 30 minutes."

When she arrived I noticed how attractive she was with moderate, very pointy, cone shaped breasts.

"So how old are you?" I asked her after she said hello.
"I'm 20 and just moved out here with my father and his family."
"Dig that; so what do u like to do?"
"I like to jog, read, and walk the dog. I'm really a home body."
"So do you drink or smoke?" I asked.
"Naw, I may have a drink or two every now and then," she responded.

We kicked it for a few hours watching movies and then she asked me to give her a massage. I decided to loosen her up with the massage she asked me for.

My heart usually beat very slowly because I was in excellent shape, but I never felt my heart react that way in my chest before like it was doing.

The minute I saw her in those little ass shorts I could feel the tip of my dick starting to thrust violently under my shorts. The pumping began to pick up very forcefully. I could tell during this massage that I was starting to get aroused by this sexy ass caramel complexioned young woman. I was hoping that she didn't bump up against my rock hard dick.

"I just really came for a massage," she said but then she started to undress. She undid her bra and panties and started to lie down on the bed on her stomach. As I began to massage her back and the back of her legs for about 15 minutes, I could feel my heart beating more violently each passing minute. I reached down between her legs. Her pussy was unshaved and very wet. I could feel her clitoris throbbing under her pussy lips with each stroke. By this time she couldn't wait for me to tell her to flip over.

She immediately turned on her back as I started to massage her stomach. She glided my hands around to her pussy that was still covered by her panties. I looked at her breasts. They were actually blowing up with each incredible, forceful beat of her heart. I could see them filling up the cup of her bra and turning into swollen cones. I never even really showed her my hard dick, but it definitely looked like it was fully erect and trying to push out of my boxer shorts.

She was acting like she wasn't even interested in touching a man's dick let alone look at one, but I really couldn't take it anymore. I must have lost control but I made a grab for my dick and pulled my shorts down.

From the look on her face I could tell that it was big and beautiful, but it seemed to make her a little nervous. When my dick gets hard it's about 9 and a half inches long. "Why you got those big ass veins all through it? Why your balls so hairy and big?" I laughed as she began to caress my hard dick.

I could feel my shit throbbing in her small hands and that got me even more aroused as she softly touched my dick and balls. I watched her jerk my shit up and down. I knew at this point she wanted me so I ripped her bra and panties off her body. I couldn't believe her breasts could get that big and pointy, and my heart was beating like I had just ran five miles uphill.

While she stroked my shit I began to lick her breasts. It was incredible. I once again felt her clitoris. It was throbbing out of control so violently that it felt like it was going to leap out of her pussy. I really enjoyed what happened next. It felt so great pushing my dick inside her as I started to thrust back and forth. It felt so good as her warm pussy kept locking on my shit as I went back and forth inside her. I wanted to pull it out but I couldn't. I didn't want to get her pregnant but the pleasure was unbearable.

I lifted her legs as she began to try to wrap them around me. I kept trying to spread her legs wider, hoping my shit would go even deeper in her. After about 35 minutes of my powerful fucking, I could feel the muscles in her body tighten and that was when I knew she was having an orgasm.

I then thought I could give the female body worlds of pleasure. I could feel my shit start to nut inside her. It was so warm. I then began thinking, "Damn, I just nut in this bitch!" as I started to withdraw my dick out of her pussy. At that point it was too late to worry about it.

Chapter 10

Cali, Great Place to Visit

Then one late summer night, we were hanging out watching movies and eating pizza. Being the gentleman that I am, I escorted Camille home down the block and up the hill discussing what our lives and the future may hold. We both wanted this summer fling to turn into a relationship. I was also hoping to get me some but Aunt Joyce wasn't having it that night she was on security watch so nothing was happening there. When Camille put the key in the door to get inside her father snatched the door open. He was standing waiting with a shotgun and ready to grill her on whom I was and where had she been.

"What's your name?" he asked me with the shotgun pointed to my face.

My mind went blank for a quick second as I stared at this greasy, grizzly bear looking motherfucker. The only thing I could think of to say was, "My name is Michigan."

"Well Michigan you got 10 seconds to get out of here before I blow your ass away," said her father.

Before he could finish the sentence I abruptly turned and ran away. I ran so fast I had passed Uncle Hollywood's house, then I realized I had gone too far.

I stopped to catch my breath and ran back up the hill back to Unk's house. I went inside and told them how this crazy man had pulled a shotgun on me. I was stunned and didn't know what to do.

To my dismay, Unk and Aunt Joyce fell out laughing at what I thought was a near death experience. I really didn't think it was that funny. The next day I wanted to see Camille but her sister stopped by while she was out walking the dog and explained how she was grounded and how their over protective and old school dad was. These were grown women but they had curfews.

After that night I continued to see Camille and we had a steady relationship for three months. Then just like that her father sent her to live with her mother in Maryland. We kept in touch for a while but after like a month or so the calls stopped. I did always wonder about Camille but was just unable to get back in contact with her, so I just put it in the back of my mind and started dating other chicks.

Not too long after Camille and I broke it off, I started back hollering at chicks on a regular basis. That's when I met Shannon, a 24 year old thick, redbone that was a flight attendant that was sexy as hell. I ran into her at the gas station. She had just got out her car as I was pulling into the gas station. She was wearing some tight, little, red shorts with a bikini top, and I knew I just had to say something if we crossed paths.

Yep, with some good timing we happened to be heading toward the door at the same time, so I did the gentleman thing and opening the door for her. Walking behind her I got a good view of that nice, round ass. I had to act quickly as I said, "Sweetheart, I'm not from here.

Can you tell me how to get to the mall from here?" She looked shocked at first but then seemed to come around as she began trying to explain how to get downtown where the mall was located.

"Look sweetheart, can you just show me the way if you have time? I'd make sure you're compensated for your time."

"Well, I was on my way home and I do live out that way so I guess you can follow me. I'm gonna' go straight and you'll go left when we get to the downtown exit, ok?"

"Yeah, but how will I give you the compensation for your help?"

"I'm good. I have to go that way anyway, so thanks, but no thanks."

"Well the least you can do is let me take you out to eat one day. That is if your man don't mind," I said seeing if I could pick her brain.

"Naw, he won't mind because he don't exist," she responded.
I laughed to myself thinking, that shit works every time. "Well, since you won't go to the mall with me, can I at least get a number to call you then?"

"No, but I'll take yours though."

"Sweetheart, I told you I'm not from here and I don't know my uncle's number."

"Well, I guess this can't happen then because I'm not giving you my number!"

"Ok, I got my uncle's other cell phone. I don't know the number but if you let me call your phone then you'll have it. How does that sound?"

"Ok I'll do that. Where is the phone?"

"It's in my car. Let me run and get it real quick."

"Ok fine but please hurry up."

After we did the phone hookup I followed her to my stop and then to the mall. After a few weeks of talking to Shannon on the phone I thought she was a goody, goody two shoes, church girl, so I didn't put any moves on her in an attempt to respect her religion.

One night we were watching TV on the couch when my uncle said they were going to bed. About 15 minutes later Shannon started to passionately kiss me and whispered to me, "You know what I want?" I sure did. We made out and petted for a few more minutes when she said she was going to the bathroom and I was to meet her in the guest bedroom. When she walked into the room we wasted no time in frantically tearing off each other's clothes. I took my throbbing dick and placed it between her damp thighs and slowly stroked it back and forth, getting us even hotter.

Without further ado, I took her by the hand and led her to the bed, gently pushed her onto her back, and slipped my dick into her gushing, wet pussy. I started to bang away without abandon. It didn't take long before she couldn't take my pounding anymore and she let out a whimper and shuddered beneath me in a wild orgasm.

This sent me over the edge and I filled her pussy with my semen, my back arching in passion as I did so. We spent the next several hours trying out nearly every possible sexual position before finally calling it a night!

One Sunday afternoon my uncle's friend Jeff came by to see if I wanted to go to the gym and hoop for a few hours, I quickly accepted his offer and went to the gym with him. There were about 30 guys there ready to ball including a few friends and acquaintances of Jeff.

You could tell that most of the guys were businessmen and guys that had definitely played some college and professional ball because of the level of ball they played. I was just doing like I always do. Being myself on the court, getting buckets, setting people up, and playing good defense.

After playing for like two hours we finished, I was talking to this older gentleman and he gave me his card and told me to call him on Wednesday around 1:00 in the afternoon. I took the card and figured I'd do just that.

I still was not sure who he was and what he did, but just figured he wanted me to play ball with them again, so when Jeff and I got in his car he asked me did I know the cat I was talking to. That's when Jeff told me that he was David Mitchell, the assistant coach at USC, and he had played pro for 9 years overseas in Europe.

"Wow, I figured he was something because the way he played the game it was too easy and he just played different to me."

"Just before we left he asked me to bring you to work out with him at the college because he was interested in trying to sign you to a deal to play for the USC Trojans!" Jeff said with excitement in his voice.

"Playing for a division one program was always a part of my dreams."

"Well, this guy is definitely a person that can make that dream come true."

We entered the west-side freeway heading back to Unk's crib. It seemed like weeks had passed but finally Wednesday came. Time was moving really slow that morning. I kept picking up the card and the phone and putting them down thinking about what time he told me to call him.

I decided to go shower and get dressed to work out in my uncle's neighborhood fitness center down the street to try to get my mind off of this call.

After working out for a few hours it was about that time to give Mr. Mitchell a call. With mad nerves and that lump you get in your throat, I picked up the phone and dialed the number. Ring, ring, ring, ring

"Hello, USC Men Basketball Office. David Mitchell speaking, how can I help you?"

"Good afternoon sir, this is Kendrick Macklemore. I spoke with you on Sunday at the gym and you gave me this card and asked me to give you a call this afternoon," I said after a short pause.

"Oh, hey Kendrick. I'm glad you gave me a call. I was just talking about you this morning to some of the other coaches."

"Wow, I hope it was good stuff."

"Most definitely, son. I told them that we need to look into offering you a scholarship and making you a Trojan. How does that sound?"

"Sounds great to me, sir. I'd be honored to play for you guys," I said trying to hide some of the excitement in my voice.

"Ok Kendrick, can you come over to our campus tomorrow around 6pm? We have an open gym tomorrow so the coach wants to see you play against some of our players."

"I sure can, sir. I'll be there around 5:30, sir."

"Ok Kendrick, see you tomorrow."

"Yes, sir."

After putting the phone down I sat on the bed and tried to comprehend what just happened.

Then of course I called my parents and several other family and friends letting them know what just transpired. Finally, I called Shannon and asked if she could swing by because I needed to talk to her. She said cool and said to just give her a few minutes. She'd be over. She called me when she got outside and I came out and greeted her with a kiss.

"What's that for baby?" she said.

"Just because I'm lucky to have you," I said with a devilish smile.

"Yea whatever Ken. So what did you want to talk about?" she said.

"Sweetheart I got some great news today. I received a call from USC's assistant basketball coach offering me a scholarship to play basketball for them."

"Wow, that's wonderful baby. Are you gonna take it?" she asked.

"Well first I gotta work out with the team tomorrow and we'll see after that."

"You'll do great. I got faith in you," she said.

"I hope so. Well I guess that's one of the reasons I needed you to come through."

"Oh yeah? So what's the other one?" she asked with a Kool Aid smile, as I leaned in to kiss her again.

We headed to her crib to hangout. We were out in the den lying on a daybed that had been set up there. Things started heating up quickly. I was spooning her, squeezing her breasts, feeling her nipples through her shirt, and leaving hot, wet kisses on her neck. We began kissing and removing clothing almost immediately and I quickly made my way down to her steamy pussy and began sucking on her clit.

She was normally very loud and I think trying to contain it was like trying to hold back a tidal wave for her. Just as she finished coming, I moved up to kiss her, because she had told me she loved to kiss a man that tasted like her. I teased her briefly before slowly inching my dick up inside her. Her facial expression was priceless as I started pushing myself into her. She rolled me over on my back and called my name just as she was coming again.

I burst inside her but didn't go limp. I could never go completely limp with her. Both of us were still ravenous for more. I flipped her over and started fucking her doggy style, reaching around and tickling her clit while she moaned and talked dirty to me. With my come now dripping out of her hot pussy, I busted again and we collapsed.

The next day it was time to roll up to the campus of USC and my chance to change my future. It would be an understatement for me to say I was nervous as we pulled up outside their practice facility. After getting in there and preparing to play so many things was running through my head. I took a second to pray, 'Dear GOD, please allow me the ability to play my best and give my all as you keep me safe from hurt, harm, or danger while I'm on the court. Amen.'

I played extremely well. I did it all: scoring, assisting, and defending. Today was a good day I had everything working. I could see the coaches were definitely impressed as I caught a glimpse of them out the corner of my eye. Shortly after the last few games Coach Mitchell came over to me and asked me to come with him as we walked over towards the head coach and a few other assistants.

"Hey Kendrick right?" Coach Hawkins himself asked me. I was momentarily star-struck as I said, "Yes sir."

"Son we enjoyed watching you play and would love to offer you a full athletic scholarship. If you want it that is."

"Wow, I don't know what to say. This is way past my wildest dream, sir, but I'll be more than happy to accept your offer," I said with tears in my eyes.

"Okay my secretary will mail you your package here in the next few days. I look forward to talking to you real soon, Kendrick. Welcome and congratulations son, you earned it," Coach Hawkins said as he extended his hand for me to shake.

"Once again thanks, sir," I said as I shook hands with a legend. He and a few others coaches walked to his office and Coach Mitchell and I stayed behind and conversed for a couple more minutes before he joined them.

Just like Coach Hawkins said I received the scholarship package in the mail a few days after. This was also the same day of The Fila Pro Am Basketball League at the L.A. Forum was held. It was Derrick Outlaw, Jolene McCoy, Jon Wallace, Toby Bailey, two white boys that played for UCLA that I didn't know, and myself. The league was four weeks long and this was their first year playing in it, but this was the best team that they had put in it. They were looking to do some good things this year.

There were some good teams in it, like the young Lakers who won the championship, and this year's team included the newly acquired Kobe Bryant. We had local high school standouts of our own in Baron Davis so we felt good.

After the league started and was coming down to the end, we were in the hunt for securing a tournament bid. The goal seemed close enough to touch, or at least close enough to talk about. We needed wins against LA Hammers and South Central Rollers, the pro's two worst teams, to clinch a league championship in the season's final weekend. All we had to do was remain focused on each game.

Then this would be a hallmark for our team this year. True to the season's form, the wins wouldn't come easily. We needed a late three pointer by Scott Green to break a tie with the LA Hammers and help secure a 60-51 win.

The next night we survived an emotional surge in the second half with the Rollers in the final game to beat them 64-59. Securing a tournament bid did not sink in immediately, but when we got in the locker room we realized what we had accomplished.

Our starters did most of the heavy lifting in the championship run, but I did average 12 points during the run. It was a great learning experience to be a part of and have access to NBA facilities, so it wasn't hard to see other NBA superstars. I was very fortunate to be able to be in a situation like this where I watch them workout against pros and guys on their level.

It's good to get some tips from NBA players so you can see what you need to do to get to their level. The league allowed LA area fans each summer to witness extravagant and watch these past, present and future legends exhibit their talent. This event had been organized over the past 24 years with the concept that the league would add to the quality of life in the LA area and provide an alternative for family fun during the summer months.

Though my team came in second place I played pretty good I'd say. But on top of that this was a great experience that I'd never forget. Also I got to meet some NBA/WNBA superstars past, present and possibly future ones. I have to thank Uncle Hollywood for giving me the opportunity for this exposure.

Things were looking great I had a magnificent girl and the chance to play division 1A basketball but I guess that saying is true: You can take the nigga out the small city, but you can't take the small city mentally out the nigga' because believe it or not I was starting to get mad homesick and I found out that I was going to have to play two years at Clintonville Community College because I only had a GED. I had to complete one year at a community college before being able to attend a university so this put a monkey wrench in my plans. I did what I always do and ran back to the Midwest.

I asked Shannon if she could get me a ticket under her friends and family. She told me yeah and I never told her I wasn't coming back. Damn, in the words of Biggie, Cali a great place to visit. 'I'm out…'

Chapter 11

The Start of My Dope-boy Ambition

Fresh off my 9 month stay in Cali, I was back in Springfield, Michigan. It was the beginning of the summer of 98' and I still had to finish school or find a job. I had to do something with myself, so I bounced around from adult school to adult school. I just could not stay focused on getting those four credits that I still had to acquire for my high school diploma that I should have received in 95'. It was also time for the run-and-gun the city top basketball league.

For anybody that played ball from this part of city it was like our own little NBA, even if you were playing pro, semi pro, college. The Run-and-Gun was unlike any other event in the city. It was a legendary program that this small basketball town had embraced and it was my time to get back to the top of the mountain. Later that evening I was on my way to the gym to play in the summer's first adult games of the 98' summer season.

I was ready to show off some of the new moves I learned from my stay in Cali, plus I was very confident because I had been playing with, and holding my own against, very exceptional NBA, college, and street players out there.

Upon my arrival I ran into Carmen Holyfield, who I had not seen since high school about three years earlier. She stood about 5'3", had thick thighs, a nice fat ass and slim waist. With a 34DD bust, she was built.

We talked briefly before the game and I played against some guys from MCC, the community college in my city. I went on to score 59 points, eight rebounds, and six assists. I put on a complete show.

It was like being back in high school all over again. When the game was over we were all outside kicking it when Carmen sent her little cousin over to me and asked me to come over to her for a second. I followed the teenage girl to a small blue car where Carmen and her friends sat.

"Kendrick, I haven't seen you in years, where do you live?"

"I just moved back here Saturday."

"I was talking to somebody the other day and I asked them if you were dead?" she said while laughing.

"Naw, I ain't dead, as you can see" I responded slightly angry.

"So where have you being hiding?"

"I've been in Cali for like nine months and before that I was in Indiana."

She smiled again and asked if I was dating anyone. I explained that I had just gotten back into town and had not gotten around to getting back out there in the dating scene as of yet. She asked if I would take her number.

"Yeah," I responded. She gave me the number and then pulled off. I went back over to the guys and continued the conversation.

"K-mac man your game has gotten even tighter since high school," Chandler said.

I laughed and expressed my gratitude for the compliment, but I was thinking that my ball skills were just held back while in high school. We all talked for about 30 more minutes and I cut out and went to the crib. Later that evening I got a call from Carmen. She was trying to hook up and catch up on old times.

I agreed to meet her, and then got off the phone. After 15 minutes of trying to find something to wear on this extremely warm summer evening, I said fuck it and just decided on some blue jean shorts and a white wife beater with the new $200 Penny Hardaway's that had yet to hit the Midwest. Ten o'clock in the evening came around and she was pulling up to my parent's house. I came outside to meet her as she parked. We embraced as soon as she exited her car. We stood in front of the crib and talked I could feel some old feeling that I had for her back in the day and I could see that she was feeling it to. We must have talked for hours. The conversation was coming to an end as we now sat in her car. I grabbed for the door she grabbed my wrist and said, "So you're gonna' leave without giving me a goodbye kiss?"

I really wasn't expecting this so I had to think fast. Before she had arrived I had just got done eating chilidogs with onions so I had to go in the house and get some gum or mints before I attempted this kiss. What could I say? Then it hit me.

So I told her I had to go cut the water sprinklers off in the back real quick. That's when I would run in the house and use some mouthwash and grab some gum. Damn, it worked, I thought to myself afterward. I did just that and I went to the backyard. She came back there just after I had grabbed the gum and came out the house.

My timing was great. We met at the side of the house. I grabbed her and kissed her slow and soft. I could tell she enjoyed this kiss because she didn't want to stop. We continued to kiss and touch each other for about 20 minutes nonstop. I began to grab her juicy ass in them tight little red shorts, and then I started touching the pussy from the outside of her shorts. I could see her eyes roll in the back of her head. I then unbuttoned her shorts and put my hand in her panties. I felt that wet pussy and it was wetter than a motherfucker. I got rocked up on from the first feel of her pussy. I played with it and she began to moan.

That's when I asked her if she wanted to come inside. She said, "Yes, what have you been waiting on?"

We went straight to my room and started back kissing and touching. She then stood up and took off her shorts and panties. That body was banging. I pulled down my shorts. My dick was hard as hell. She walked back to me and slid my hard dick in her now dripping wet pussy.

We fucked for like an hour although it felt like we had been fucking for over two hours when we finished. It was some of the best sex I had ever had. As we were putting our clothes back on we agreed to be together from that point on.

Two years has come and gone, and Carmen and I were still together. We had our own crib and everything. This couldn't have been better until she found out she was pregnant. That's when the trouble began. She decided to have an abortion because she thought our relationship wasn't strong enough and she already had a child without a father. She didn't want to be in that position again.

Though times weren't always bad, we had some very good times over the two and a half years we spent together. But this was a real problem for me and it seemed like she was already convinced that she was not going to have my baby. Shortly after deciding this I started back to "Doing me!" I started back hollering at bitches and flirting like I did before we got involved. I was back in full effect and had a different chick every night from that point on. I did it because I was hurt and upset. I loved this woman and she didn't want to have my child, so I would vent by chasing their women and chasing them hard.

Though I continued to stay in this relationship with Carmen, I still continued to cheat and on a regular basis. Our relationship was at an all-time low and she was unhappy with her own life at the time. She started to look for other opportunities, so she started talking to an Air Force recruiter who convinced her to join the US Air Force.

When she finally joined I had mixed emotions about the whole deal, but had to keep it player, you feel me? She started to get ready for her new opportunity and I started to get ready for my own opportunity that had come my way to play for a team overseas called the Italian Cobra's. It was a three month deal. Since our relationship was going south, so I took the deal, fuck it! This was one more chance to play and get closer to playing my dream of playing in the league one day.

During Carmen's time in basic training it was hard for me because she left when we were still trying to fix our relationship. It would suffer greatly over the next three months, and for more than one reason. The first reason being that she left shit when it was bad.

The other reason was because I was getting ready to leave the country and play pro ball, so I was fucking bitches left and right before it was time for me to depart. I stopped taking her calls on a regular basis. She would load up my voicemail with messages. One day she left eight messages.

I started messing with this younger chick and little momma was bad. She was about 5'6," 127 lbs. slim but had a very sexy ass body for her age. She had a nice little round ass with sexy long legs and some pretty full breasts.

Her name was Gwen. I began dealing with her the day that Carmen had the abortion and also decided that she was going to the military. This was a day of mixed emotions' but rules to the game is never let them see you sweat.

My chick had left for the weekend on a military trip. I was going to go with her until work asked me to come in over the weekend. I was a little disgruntled about it but agreed to go in. I was relaxing on the couch the day before having to go in, watching a movie, when the doorbell rang. I got up and slowly walked to the door to answer it. I was relaxing, only wearing boxers. It was Gwen.

She said as I opened the door, "I called you a few times and got no answer so I decided to just come by."

"Yeah, well you know me and my girl live here right?" I responded.

"Yeah but I'm better for you than she and I'm here to prove it!" She nodded at me as her hand cupped my cock and balls through my boxers and lightly squeezed. I quickly brought her in and closed the door.

She followed me to the living room and we sat down. We were having a short conversation that Gwen interrupted by getting up and standing in front of me. Wearing a t-shirt and jeans, Gwen started to undo her jeans as she looked at me lustily and said, "I won't bite, unless you like that shit!"

She almost moaned as she slowly slid her pants down. This was happening way too fast, I couldn't believe she was going to try fuck me in our house. Gwen's jeans slid to the floor, she kicked them aside, standing in front of me with a tiny blue, lace thong and her t-shirt. She started teasing the waistband of her thong as she bit her lower lip.

My dick was beginning to rise despite knowing I was in the crib Carman and I shared. Gwen moved a hand over her covered pussy, slid aside the strip of fabric covering her clit, and whispered, "I need your dick Kendrick." While she rubbed my hardening dick through my boxers, I kept my eyes fixed on the front door. As she lightly ran her middle finger between her pussy lips, trying to teasing me more, she whispered lustily, "Looks like he's needs it too." She reached her hand into the slit of my boxers and pulled out my dick.

Gwen walked between my spread legs as she continued teasing her pussy with her finger. She licked her lips as she put one foot next to my hip and then stepped completely onto the couch with her feet on each side of my hips. I looked up at door again then back at her young pussy that hovered above me. "I'm getting her all wet for you," Gwen moaned in my ear.

I stuck my tongue out as I looked up at that wet pussy. She brought her pussy to my tongue as she split her lips apart with her fingers. My tongue sank into her tight hole as she pushed into me and she let out a long moan. She kept pushing into me until my nose brushed against her tiny clit. She leaned more into me, resting her upper body against the wall while covering my face.

She slowly began to move her hips up and down enabling my tongue to fuck her, grinding her clit into my nose each time they met. A short time later I wrapped my hand around my dick and began to stroke the head.

I moaned with pleasure into Gwen's, moistening. She started moving her hips faster against my face, her moans getting louder. I rubbed my finger against the tip of my dick.

Her body was shaking in pleasure as I felt her pussy squeeze on my tongue. I heard Gwen moan out, "Oh My God, I'm gonna cum." Her legs were trembling as she pushed herself into my face hard, grinding her hardened clit into my nose.

I was still stroking my dick as I encouraged her to come all over my face and to let me taste her cum. Gwen's body froze as she continued trembling, letting out a long, loud moan. Her pussy clamped down hard on my tongue as a rush of fluid quickly filled my mouth and ran down my cheeks. Gwen's body convulsed against me as her orgasm coursed through her.

As her orgasm slowly began to fade, Gwen's legs gave out and she fell to her knees in front of me, her small ass pressing against my throbbing dick. I looked at her and smiled as I cupped her ass, holding her thong aside, and lifted her up. I moved my dick forward and pulled it up. I lowered my hands as I lowered Gwen down until the head of my dick slowly slipped into her tight wet pussy.

Gwen's eyes opened wide as her pussy slowly moved onto my dick. She moved her pussy down until her ass almost touched my boxers. She was taking short, shallow breaths as she looked down at my shit going in and out of her pussy. I moved my hands to her ass again, to help her lift up and ride my dick. I hit that pussy like that for 20 to 30 minutes before she turned around and backed towards me. I watched her as she grabbed my dick, rubbing the head against her clit.

As Gwen continued to rub my dick against her clit, I grabbed her hips and aimed her up to my dick, which was now spreading her pussy lips open.

With a little force I began to pull her onto my dick. Gwen threw her head back as my dick slowly penetrated her pussy again. I pulled her down until her ass rested against my abdomen, my dick throbbing in her contracting pussy.

Gwen leaned back against me and whispered, "Oh fuck, that feels good." With her feet planted on the floor, she pressed her back against my chest, lifting her hips up slowly. I looked at Gwen and her eyes closed as I was using my thumb on her clit, rubbing it hard and whispering nasty shit to her. Gwen's ass was slapping against my thighs hard as she slammed down onto me moaning, "Oh God I'm gonna cum, I'm gonna cum."

A few minutes later, Gwen started riding my dick hard, pressing into my chest hard each time she lifted up, whispering, "God I love your dick." I reached between her legs to find her enlarged clit, again, and I started running my fingers up and down against it. I groaned, "That's it you dirty slut, ride my big dick." She started grunting each time she slammed her ass into me, her legs trembling. Soon after that I heard Gwen yell out, "Yes, I'm coming, daddy!"

"You're making me cum too, damn it."

Gwen's body was trembling, completely down on my dick, as juices started to flow out soaking my abdomen as I said, "That's it baby, cum all over daddy's dick." My dick throbbed hard in Gwen's pussy as she tried to speak. I put my hands on her hips to get her to fuck me again.

She resisted, still trying to get herself together from the nut she just busted. Gwen's orgasm slowly faded as she lay against me, breathing heavily. I rubbed her back, allowing her a chance to recover.

Ten or fifteen minutes passed as Gwen started riding my dick again, with the same speed as before. She laid her head against my shoulder and whispered, "Make me come, Kendrick. Make me come again, please." I started rubbing her clit rapidly as I urged her on.

"Yes baby, cum all over daddy's dick. Fuck me until you make yourself come." I flipped her over as I got down on my knees in front of her. I pulled her to me so her ass hung over the edge of the couch. I spread her legs apart and guided my dick back into her. With one or two swift pushes, I buried half of my dick into her pussy once more. For the fourth time Gwen's body started shaking hard as she made her movements more forceful into me.

"I'm gonna come Kendrick! My pussy's gonna come on your big hard dick," she moaned loudly.

I frigged her clit hard, groaning, "That's it cum on my big hard dick." She slammed into me hard as her pussy squeezed my dick harder. She yelled out as her body thrashed against me, her orgasm rocking her body. Her hips lifted up as her pussy forced my dick out of her, followed by a stream of juices. Her hips bucked hard again as she rubbed her clit, shooting more juices out of her pussy. I grabbed my shit as I threw my head back as she let out a long growl. While Gwen was coming down off her climax I started moaning out.

"Oh shit, yes I'm coming now. Open up your month, and let daddy's nut fill you up."

You could see my dick throb as she growled again, jerking it. I looked at her and whispered, "Ready for more cum?" She nodded while moaning, "Yes give it all to me." I shot more cum into her mouth.

As I finished shooting cum all in her mouth and on her face, I collapsed on the floor next to her, breathing heavily with a freaky grin on my face. I stood up again and fell back on the couch exhausted, slowly drifting off to sleep.

Although me and Carman decided to patch up our relationship before she actually left for her basic training, I had now opened up this thing with Gwen and was kinda in over my head.

But I knew all that was needed to do was get through one week. Easier said than done but if I had to pick a nigga to do it, that would be me… After that week had passed and I managed to see both women and not get caught up, that is when Carmen asked me to help move her things Kentucky. Damn this definitely through a monkey wrench in my plan. But once again I'd see my way through it, so I told Gwen that the team I was going away to play for needed me to come to Kentucky for a week long camp. She bought it and I was good to go, then I was able to make both women happy. Your boy got skills.

During the road trip with Carmen there were a lot of conversations about us trying to work out our problem and to go on and have a productive life. We both share some things that we did during the relationship. Airing our dirty laundry, so to speak. After about seven hours of driving and talking she fell fast to sleep. So in the time that my girl slumbered I began to figure out how I was going to break it off with Gwen.

See this too sounded easier than was gonna be, but if I wanted Carmen back like I claimed then I'd better break off this fling sooner than later.
Ten in a half hours later we made it to Good Ridge, KY. So we grabbed a hotel room at the Holiday Inn for the night. See Carmen and I, we had sex everywhere and any time we could. I really liked public places and she didn't care. Shit was absolutely fantastic.

See this time was unlike any other because her mother and family had accompanied us on this moving trip to help and one of her relatives drove the U-haul. So she looked at me before we got in the room and told me to follow her to the bathroom. She went into the bathroom. I went and looked at the U-haul and stuff, and to see what her people was doing. They were at the Denny's across the parking lot so I rushed back to the room.

When I went into the bathroom she was already necked. I quickly kissed her and started sucking on her nipples. She was moaning by this point. I licked my way down her body and drove my tongue into her hot wet pussy. She was swaying on her feet. I licked and sucked at her clit till she came hard and got my face all wet.

I stood up and she immediately went to my shit and lowered my zipper and took my dick in her mouth. She sucked on me for a while. She stopped and put her leg up on the sink and told me to hit that pussy. I worked my big black dick into her and after a few try's on I was balls deep. We fucked like that for about 15 minutes.

She then told me she wanted me in her ass. We'd never done this before, but I was game. I got some of her pussy juice and some lotion she carried and lubed her up and slid my shit in her back door slowly.

Once I got in, I fucked her hard. She was moaning and gasping with every pump. Just after I came, we heard a knock at the door.

"WHAT'S GOING ON IN THERE?" one of her relatives shouted through the door. She yelled, "Nothing. I am just about done." We cleaned ourselves up and I left the bathroom first. Five minutes later she came out, wearing nothing but her robe. It was definitely a great relaxer after a long road trip…

I met this nigga in the military through my cousin Glen. He was like a captain or some shit, but he was cool as fuck. He started buying weed from me so we clicked up and began communicating on the regular. He would keep me posted on what Carmen was doing and whom she was seeing, until she hooked up with his friend and they started talking. That's when the nigga started acting "brand new." But it was all good because I met this down ass chick.

It was a fine Saturday afternoon. I roamed around Mercer Street downtown Springfield and eventually walked into a small shop called Caribbean's, which was new in the city. On the windows, innovative Christmas designs were displayed that had caught my attention. The store looked deserted so I decided to step inside and buy gifts to wish my girlfriend a happy holiday since shit between us had been bad.

Chapter 12

Drama Come's With the Territory

As I entered the air, conditioned store and found a variety of skirts, halter tops, tank tops, thigh highs, and thongs. A sexy brown haired woman stood behind the counter, reading an Allure magazine. Baby was banging standing about 5'6" and weighing 140 pounds, 34-24-40 with a phat ass to match. Her long wavy hair was shoulder length, and she wore a white tube top that left her flat stomach bare. She seemed to be the only worker that day. I was staring dead at her, as I asked, "So sweetheart, what is your name? "Cedrieka," she answered. "May I help you?"

"I'm just looking for a gift for my mother and sister."

"Okay well let me know if I can help you," she said.

"By the way you can. My sister about your weight and height, so if you could try on a few sets of bikinis, swimsuit, and lingerie. I could tell how it would fit on her." She hesitated for a moment and then went on to do so. After trying on a few outfits I choose three and gave her one as I asked her for her phone number in the process.

She agreed and we exchanged numbers. After talking on the phone for a few days I pegged her as being shy, but following our first date I found she was far from shy. She was hood independent, sexy, and strong willed chick.

Even though she was a hood chick she still had other good qualities. The things that I thought would make her a better woman, made us grow closer together.

But mainly, because I still had feelings for Carman that couldn't let go. I mean, who wouldn't? Since she had been in the military, her body was lookin right! But so was

Cedricka's...Damn, what is a nigga to do? I thought to myself.

"Bae, how much you make today?" I asked her. She had her head down, like she was thinking. "Like $250." She smiled with those moon shaped dimples.

I tilted her chin with my index finger and kissed her passionately with thought of money on my mind. "Look that money is all yours. Here is a f of an ounce. I cut it up for you. It should be like $1,300 in $20 dollar ks." I said.

"Okay daddy! How much I gotta give you and by when?

"No worries just break my off $800."

"Fasho daddy!" See every time Cedrieka called me daddy it made me ny. And my dick was tellin me to just pick her up, and fuck her right re, in the kitchen. Yep right on the counter. When we were together, 'd be down for some kinky shit like that, she down for whatever. Though vas tempting I cut out because I had some other business to attend we'd •bably fuck later. Ultimately I'd called Cedrieka when I was done for the v and told her I was coming through, she agreed and I headed south bond vard her crib.

Soon as I got there we went upstairs and she immediately laid down her king size bed and sprawl out. I crawled up top of her kissing her mach, chest, and then mouth. She wrapped her hands around my neck and sed me back. She immediately took off her shirt and bra. So I quickly ked on those nice nipples.

Cedrieka then helped me unzip my pants and took down my boxers l gave me a blowjob. I immediately took my shirt and she lay back down I I took off her pants and panties and went down on her.

Cedrieka was moaning as I licked her nice clit. I reached up and ched her nipples as I continued to her suck her pussy. Cedrieka then led me up kissed me and said "I'm ready." I went to grab a rubber and drieka smiled and said "No! You're good." I immediately pushed my dick ide, we started grinding hard. As I fucked her, I grabbed her massive tits l Cedrieka said "Please keep doing that shit." I kissed her neck and lips, drieka had deep brown eyes and I could tell she was really enjoying it.

Because she slapped my ass and said "I want to ride this big dick." e changed positions and she rode me hard. That pussy was so wet, as she ced her hands on my chest, so I pulled her down and kissed her again. drieka then sat up, continued to fuck me and had her hands her hands in r hair when I told Cedrieka I was cumming.

She said ok and continued fucking me and she said "Its ok, I'm on the l." I gripped the bed sheets and bust my nut all inside her.

Cedrieka took my entire nut and immediately fell on me then kissed e. She then asked, "I hope you have more in you." And I said, "I plan on ving a lot more for next time." We laughed and Cedrieka said."I'm about take a shower." Which I said "No doubt."

117

As she got up and I could see my cum dripping out and Cedrieka said, "Damn, you must not have jacked off today? That was a huge nut."
I said,
"Well, my guess is that the next one will be much less." She smiled and said
"Good, I don't want to choke on it."

Cedrieka and I kicked it for like 7 or 8 months before things began to get a little rocky. She was starting to hear about my girl Carman and how some times when I'd be away from the city how I was with Carman. See this was on top of all the other bitches I was fucking in the city. This was different for me because I thought Cedrieka was unlike the rest of the chicks I've been involved with but after you get closer to any female they are all the same, I tell you. She was definitely gonna show it.

Things were all good but now, it's like she changing and shit. This one day she pushed me off hard when I tried to kissed her. "Ken, stop it, you so fuckin selfish!" she said, as she put her phone down as she cried and shit.

I hated when Cedrieka cry to be honest, but this was new because she was a hard ass bitch! But it's like, lately she cried too much. I just don't understand her ass anymore. "What you crying for?" I asked her. I was still looking around the house; I knew I heard a nigga voice on the phone as she quickly got off the phone just before I came in the room. See I'd kill any nigga Cedrieka fuck wit, and I hope she knew that shit. No next nigga about to ever think it's cool to fuck my bitches. Well at least not money getter, me and her got an understanding, but I'm not fixing to accept that shit from Cedrieka.

"I'm so tired of you and all yo shit! First, you bring yo ass over here after you been fucking with that bitch all day, now you tryna fuck me, like c'mon now. How dumb do you think I am?!" she said.

During this time, Carman and Cedrieka were the only two females who I had soft spots for. I swear they were the only bitches I had feelings for. I always felt like I had to be there for them. I had to protect them both. It wasn't right I was the one making Cedrieka cry. "Alright, I'm sorry." I pulled her in my arms for a hug. Though I still wanted to fuck her, but I was tired of us having beef. I kissed her forehead.

She was still crying though. I guess she must've been in a lot of pain.

"Ken, we not supposed to be like this. Whether we together or not, I don't want us being so hostile toward each other. We need to make sure we can at least be civil, right?" She looked up at me.

Cedrieka bad as fuck I swear, she don't even have to try to be cute.

"Yeah, you right. I love you, okay?"

"I love you too Ken but I know you in love with Carman, I ain't stupid!" she said.

"Dig that, I can't lie your on point but I really do love you too. But I'm glad we had this talk though." I said to her. She nodded her head. I knew this was the end of Cedrieka's and my relationship. We managed to get along better and we continued to get money as we became business partners. We were getting along for the first time since we broke up.

Future players need to understand that emotions can get involved and they can overplay their hand. These emotions can change the dynamics of a relationship. Damn sometime life can be a bitch!

See with all this shit going on at this time I lost focus on my hustle, and I'd take a major loss. It was the average day. I hit up my manz, Max, and told him I needed to grab 2 ounces that when he asked me to meet him at his crib. I agreed and we met about 30 minutes later and did the exchange. See I never question dude because of two reasons. First, because shit was always straight, and secondly, my mind was all fucked up over these hoes. This I didn't see coming. Soon as I got to the crib I called up Max one of my crack heads was who I liked to use for testing my dope. Second after he put it in his crack pipe and took a hit he said, "K-mac you better get yo' money back." Fuck I just lost $1500!

That's what I was thinking. I decided to lay low for a little while to develop a new strategy because this shit isn't supposed to happen to me. After a few months of unsuccessful attempts of trying to complete high school I said fuck it and bought a half ounce of weed for $50. I made $115 dollars few days. I quickly turned that same $115 into $230 in four more days of hustling, so after about a month I was able to buy a quarter pound. I thought I was getting back.

I continued to sale weed and chase women on a day to day basis until one day my favorite cousin Jada and her boyfriend Ramón came for a visit. They lived in The Wood. I loved when they would come to town because we had the best times. They would always want to get some Big Cheese pizza. It was the best pizza in the world to us. Jada was light skinned, about 5'3" and 135 pounds, and always wore her hair different because she was a hair stylist. I must add my cousin was a very beautiful woman like all the women in my family.

This particular time she came we had so much fun they asked me to go back with them for like a week or so, and Ramón offered to bring me back home whenever I was ready. I went because Ramón was a cool nigga and he had a younger brother name Major that I fucked with.

Major and Ramón were like night and day. Ramón was a barber that went to work every day like clockwork. He wasn't always a good guy.

He was locked up for like seven years, but after he came home he changed his life for the best. Major on the other hand was just the opposite. He did four years and got out and got worst. This was a hustling ass nigga whom sold everything. He could sell water to a whale. Ice in the winter, fire in hell. I clicked with both of them because I looked up to them, but Ramón was my good angel and Major was the little red devil. Major was a good nigga though. He was very smart and well-spoken just like his big brother "Money-Món." That is what Ramón's nickname was when he was a hustler.

On my visit to The Wood it was unlike any other time. For some reason it was like Drug School 101 and Major was the teacher that was about to teach me everything I needed to know about the dope game. One early Monday morning Major woke up and said, "Are you gonna roll with me or Ramón and Jada?"

"I'm going to hang with you if that's cool with you?" I responded.

"Yeah that's what's up."

We went riding around until we stopped on a one way street. He got out and ran up to this apartment. He returned in like 15 minutes and then we drove off. He went into his pants and came back out with a brown paper bag. He tossed it over to me and asked me to count it for him, saying it should be like $12,000.

"Yeah, ok." I responded calmly but in my head I was like, "Damn! $12,000? What the fuck." I counted the money, put it back in the paper bag, then put it in the glove box. A minute after that we arrived to a second house were we both went in.

This crib was laid out. It had everything a big screen television with the new Play Station, leather furniture, and a pool table in the dining room back near where the bedroom was located. I sat patiently on the tan leather sofa and I heard his voice call my name before he asked me to come. I headed to the back room and he was in the closet. When he came out he tossed a large plastic bag onto the bed and asked me,

"Do you know what that is?"

"Fasho, that's a pound of weed right" I quickly answered.

"Yeah," he laughed. "I got to go handle some business. Can you sit here for me?"

"Yeah, sure I can do that."

He they gave me the rules and strategy on how his house was operated then he left out the side door and jumped into his black Mustang putting the pedal to the metal.

After he screeched off, I just sat in the living room playing John Madden 1998 on the Sony Play Station and chilling when there was a knock at the door.

"Who is it?" I yelled as I grabbed the .45 caliber gun under the sofa and swiftly walked to the door. There were two cute redbones at the door. One was wearing an o-dog and tennis dress.

The other had on daisy dukes with a halter top. I cracked the door and said, "What y'all need?"

"Two of those $10 dollar green t-shirts?" This meant $10 dollar bags. I let them in and they sat on the sofa while I got the marijuana for them. One of the young ladies asked to use the bathroom. As I began to let her know where it was located she laughed and let me know she knew where it was. I sat back on the sofa across from the other female and started to play the game again. I was playing for a few minutes or so then I paused the game to get up. I went to the back bathroom with the .45 and opened the door. The young lady was in there masturbating on the toilet.

"Bitch what are you doing?" I asked violently. This chick went on to say that when I let them inside that she got wet as hell and had to get one off. While she was telling me this she never stopped masturbating. She called me closer. I moved closer, she grabbed my belt buckle and unbuckled it and my pants. In my head I was thinking a lot of things including if they were trying to stick me up. I guess this wasn't a stick up though.

She started licking and sucking all over my big, juicy dick. I was moaning so loud her girl asked, "Are y'all alright?" "Bitch, come see?" her friend yelled back. She came back and saw us going at it like two rabbits on the bathroom floor.

"Hoe, join us," her friend said.

She started to peel off her clothes and joined us. This shit was crazy. I had never been with two women at once before. This was definitely a first. We moved from the bathroom to the bedroom, sucking and fucking the whole way. We were in the room going all out having wild freaky sex. The kind that makes toes curl up and hair sweat out, frizz up and makes you look like you lost a fight with a blow dryer. Then I saw an image of a man standing in the room. I reached for the pistol and a voice said,

"Nigga, why you fucking my bitches?"

I looked up and it was Major. When I responded, "These hoes fucking me," he laughed and walked out of the room. I got up and went to the living room where he was. We talked quickly and he left again. I went back to the room and these hoes were in the shower.

After they finished showering they left and I returned to my game. I was just about to complete my game until another knock was at the door. Once again I yelled, "Who is it?" It was an older gentleman who answered he wanted a $15 dollar t-shirt. I opened the door and let him in give him his hookup. This process continued for the rest of the day. By 9:00 p.m. Major was walking in asking how did we do.

"We made like $800."

"That's all you playboy."

He picked up the joystick and asked me to run a game real quick. We played a game then locked up the house and left. He asked if I wanted to get something to eat. I said, "Yeah," so we rolled to IHOP and picked up some food and shot to the crib.

On the way to the crib he told me not to say shit about the house if my cousin asked where we had been today. I shook my head in agreement, and he added that the house was my spot and I was the new tree man. I again shook my head in agreement.

"Is this something you want to do?" he asked me.

"Fasho."

Right then and there I was now a real dope boy.   Day two was just getting used to sitting in a spot all day really training and staying focused on the hustle and only just the hustle. The first lesson I learned was that same old American gangster saying, "Don't get high off your on supply." This was a rule that everybody knew but a lot of cats seldom used. The second thing was the harder you worked the more you'll get out of the game. This shit is not something you just play around in you can lose your life behind hustling in these streets.

The third thing that came my way was to be on point at all times and be ready to live and die with your actions and decisions because you have to make irrationally ones sometimes in this game. Number four, there was no honor, nor love, in this lifestyle. A nigga will kill you over a penny or sometimes less. Don't trust anybody! Lastly, this SHIT AIN'T NO GAME! This was a real million dollar business and street level dealers were very small but at important piece.

You must understand your place, and only the strong survives. These are just some of the things I picked up over for the few days of hustling. I applied them all and by weeks end I was sitting on $2,000 dollars and a half pound.

With this new and quick success I got greedy. I wanted it all and decided to shoot for it all, so that meant I had to open up the market and expand my business. So I needed to go out and get a crew.

Just one night me and big cousin was out riding around and chilling and Major said, "There go Henry bald head ass going into the barber shop, I being looking for his punk ass!" so we pull over at the shop and hop out.

"Aw right, fool where my money at?" Henry an older bald man then said, "Nigga I got yo' money right here I ain't ducking you!" then turn right back around and said "Can I win some of that money back or are you scared?" Major nodded as to indicate yeah.

So we headed to the back of the barber shop threw a door and then down some stairs and there was a pool table with a sheet over it, and about seven to eight guys shooting craps. Henry and Major both jump right in the game and win all the other guys money and now it's just the two of them that was left in the game from three hours earlier.

Major lifted the dice from the table and ask "What they do it just me and you nigga?" "Whatever you want." Henry replied pulling out a stack of bills from his pocket. "You ever shoot craps, Ken?" Major ask me winking his eye. I shook my head, yeah I fuck's with it. "Here" as he toss me the dice. I could see Henry protesting by the look on his face as he displayed a mouthful of shining gold teeth and then saying. "What kind of shit is this?" "His dice, chump!" Major said while dropping a twenty dollar bill on the table. "You gonna fade him or what?" "Yeah, I'll fade him." Henry then matched the twenty-dollar bill that was already on the table.

I threw the dice and they hit the wall of the table a little too hard and bounced off of the table and landed on the floor..."NO DICE, MAN!!!" Henry was angered grabbing one of the dice.

Major retrieved the other dice and returned to the now crowed table. "Dog, toss them a little softer this time. My palms perspired as I squeezed the dice once more. Once again I pitched the dice toward the table wall, this time much softer. The two small dice bounced off the table before kissing the table's wall gently. One dice showed six immediately, while the other spun momentarily before landing on five. "Eleven." Major said snatching one of the twenty from the table. Henry threw another twenty on the table and everyone looked at me. "Lick his ass again, nigga!" Major encouraged. I threw the dice again. A four and a three. "Seven." Major picked another twenty up. "GO" Henry said while throwing another bill on the table. I threw the dice again.

Both landed on two "Four." the older cat yelled as he dropped two more twenties on the table. "Forty he miss it, four the point." Major dropped two twenties down. And said "go get it for us Ken!" I nodded. "Let me get some of that?" this cat name KING said while dropping two tens on the table which Major quickly matched. I threw the dice. Eight. I threw them again. Eleven. Five. Nine. "Four!" Major yelled "don't nobody move but me!

As I rolled a four on the fifth roll, then he all the money from the table but not before dropping a single twenty back down. Henry took off his shirt and threw it across his shoulder, exposing his jail house tattoo's scars, and bullet wounds.

Henry reaches for his full wad and held it in his hand. "What it do?" He then reach into his wad and threw a fifty dollar bill on the table.

I took a deep breath as I watched Major drop a second twenty along with a ten. I unconsciously shook the dice in my hand, anxious to roll them again. "Go head, lil dog." Old school barked. I stepped to the table with ton of confidence, then threw the dice. "Ten." Henry threw two more fifty's on the table. "Let me get thirty of that." King chimed in. Major matched both men bets.

I rolled another 10 right back on his ass. "Let's go youngest." He said threw fifty on the table. "You gonna have to break me!"

I rolled a seven. Twenty minutes later, Henry wad had been diminished to two twenty dollar bills "Fade him, King!" old school was furious. "Bullshit!" King said wearing a L.A . Dodgers fitted cap. "That lil bastard on fire. He done already hit yo' ass. "I'm done." "Coward ass Muthafucka!" Henry called King, who was now heading for the door. "Go!" He threw his last money on the table. I was feeling light headed as I grabbed the dice and shook them in my hand. "Break his ass." Major stood over me holding all of Henry's money. I rolled the dice again. Eleven. Old school was finished. Major snatched the money from the table while Henry stared at me. If looks could kill, he would be murdered. The beaten man stormed from the barber shop without another word. "How do you feel?" Major asked, "About what?" I responded "about breaking up the dice game!" he added and enthusiastically counted the winnings.

"Man, you were on fire." Major separated a roll of twenties from the stack and gave them to me.

"Nigga you didn't miss a point." I counted the twenties quickly. There were 55 of them. Then I put them in my pocket before leaving the back room of the barbershop. Returning to the front Major was cut off by two Hispanic chicks dressed in Baby Phat pants and blue T-shirts I stood a couple of feet behind Major as the three of them conversed.

"It's about 4:30 now." Major checked his watch. "Hit me up in like an hour." The two Hispanic's spoke briefly in Spanish.

"About 6:30?" The taller Hispanic held up six fingers to Major. "Call me, and it was on." "Aw right, peoples catch y'all later." Major said as he headed to the door of the barber shop. And then I heard a voice woman say, "Come here" and motioning in my direction."

"Who me?" I asked. "Yeah you." Pumpkin, is now speaking to me. So I slid between Major and another cat, then approached the barber station. "How old are you?" she asked. "Twenty." I answered. Pumpkin smiled in disbelieve as she handed me her card. "One of these nights when you feel like getting away call me, you can chill at my house." "OKAY!!" I stammered. "See you later sexy." "Bye." Pumpkin said while waving. "I see you, playa," Major said as we finally left out the shop's door. I could only smile as I followed Major out the front door.

Riding in the Mustang, the thoughts of what I was going to do to Pumpkin started crossing my mind on top of this extra $1,100 I just hit a lick for. Now it was time to focus on building a bomb ass crew and taking over the streets, it was I was thinking.

Chapter 13

Puttin' My Name On The Game

My first crew consisted of me, The Boss, Prince, a 19 year old slick talking con man, Tyrone, age 18, and Buck Wild, also known as Tre-Killer. There was 18 year old Jamal, a pretty boy always on the ladies, Darius, age 17, and the down for whatever guy. We called him Lil' Dee. I taught them everything they knew about the game and put them to work. I did just that. They got money and then got a whole lot of it for me and my crew.

We had half of the south side on lock. In about just two and a half months, that same $2,000 dollars and half pound tripled. I looked at the $6,000 dollars cash money plus my crew was eating well. It was the middle of the summer and my big cousin and I was coming back from Ohio. He asked me, "Are you happy with the money you're getting?" I said, "Its good, all my niggas' straight." He lit his cigarette, took a drag and said, "How would you like to make four times what you're making now in less time?" I hesitated and then I answered, "Hell yeah, I'd love that but how is that possible?"

"I got something for you but you need to have a goal in mind before you get in this shit though. So know up front how much money you're trying to get is always the start. Do you know how much you want? If you don't have a goal it'll be almost like chasing your tail. So the first step is to decide how much you want. Give me a number."

"$25,000!" I answered.

"Are you sure?"

"Yeah, I'm sure. If I can make that I'll be straight. I'm done."

"Okay, we will see."

A couple of days after that we were at his spot on the south side where my drug lesson really got a jumpstart. He showed me everything, from the way you cook it, cut it, weigh it, and bag it. I was taught how to break down a whole kilogram of cocaine, ounce by ounce and gram by gram. I believe I was being schooled by the best and I knew there was no turning back. Later on that day I went back to my spot and called all of my crew in for an afternoon set down where I showed them just about everything I had just learned.

Over the next few weeks my team was doing crazy numbers. Something like $1,500 a day, seven days a week. That's like $10,500 a week. Damn, we were getting money so fast I had to buy a bigger space. The older hustlers in the city got jealous and started hating on us because we were getting, in their opinion, all the money and all the bitches. It was a Thursday night and Prince and I was out and checking traps and looking for bitches. It was a very slow night.

"Let's go up to the local sports bar. It'll be jumping on Thursday nights," P said.

"Fuck it, let's go," I said.

We shot over to the east side to the Heart & Soul Sports Bar. Once we were inside, I asked P if he wanted to shoot a game of pool. He said yes and went to the bar to buy a drink. I headed to the pool tables, grabbed a stick, racked the balls and went to work. Shortly after, P picked one out for himself.

I was rocking a black Detroit hat, black and white Pella sweat suit with black Air Max 90's and a gold necklace with the diamond cross and watch. I was looking like one of them NBA cats and everybody in the club was peeping us.

We were shooting a game of pool when this dark skinned, thick ass waitress came over to us and said two women sitting in a nearby booth were sending over the drink she placed in front of me. She then laughed and walked away until I requested her to come back.

"What's so funny?"

"You sexy as hell, and if those bitches wasn't all on yo' dick I would give you my number."

"Dig that, so you still can, baby girl," I said. She leaned over and was all too obvious about peeping my dick size out before she slipped me them digits on a napkin and walked off slow and sexy as fuck. Shortly after, the two women that sent me the drink came over.

The taller one who was wearing a skin tight, white bodysuit said, "Damn baby, you could have thanked us for the drink."

"My bad, sexy, I was trying to finish my game first, then I was coming over there to thank you," I responded.

"Well, my name is Marsha and this is Trisy,"

"So what's up with y'all?"

"Shit, trying to see what you got up?"

"Hold on, this my last shot."

I shot in the eight ball and told "P" it was time to jet. I had these two hoes on deck.

"Which one for me?" he asked me.

"Nigga, it doesn't matter. We fucking both of these bitches!"

Trisy's tits were firm and so was her ass. They both looked succulent with that mocha skintight, spandex dress she was wearing.

"Man, these hoes are a trip, P. They want to fuck because we getting this money," he said.

"Big homey, so what? When have you given a fuck about that shit before? Let's fuck these bitches like we always do."

We were rolling out to P's spot. Upon arrival Trisy and I tore into each other like two wild animals. She threw her arms around me and pulled my tongue deeper into her mouth. I knew she wanted me bad. I pulled her dress up over her hips and lifted her ass onto the bed.

I pushed her farther on the bed and started ripping at her dress, pulling both straps down at the same time so I could get to them big ass nipples. She took one hand and pulled my pants down from the rear. She said, "I want some dick and I want it bad!" I did just that. I opened her legs and fucked her real good from the front. I turned her around and hit that shit from the back.

She was enjoying the hell out of the dick. I called for P to come in the room. He and Marsha's tall, fine ass entered the room. I told Trisy to tell them how good the dick was while I was still fucking her. She moaned out, "Marsha, this dick is so damn good you got to try this shit bitch!"

Marsha started biting her bottom lip and rubbing her hand on her now wet pussy. Then she licked the back of my neck and went down my spine. She got to my nuts while I was still beating Trisy from the back. This other hoe was licking my balls asking me to fuck her, so I switched up the woman. I was fucking Marsha now and I told P to fuck the other bitch. He pulled down his jeans, got behind Trisy, and started hitting that shit. I slid Marsha over next to Trisy and was beating that pussy right next to him. Both of them had their asses up for us hood niggas. We were fucking side by side.

After a few minutes P let off all over that hoe's back. About 20 minutes later I told both chicks to turn around, and I exploded all over their faces. That shit was funny. I was out. When I got to the crib my girl kept calling and paging me. I told her I would get with her in the morning. I got outside to my black on black Yukon Denali and drove out north. Upon my arrival at my apartment complex I was pulled over by a sheriff for making a left hand turn without signaling, but it was just some bullshit because his first question was, "Where are the drugs and guns?"

"I don't have neither so why am I really being pulled over?"

"I ask the questions here, boy."

I knew it was a set up because of his first question and the fact mad niggas were hating on me and my crew because we were coming up like the mob. I had a lot of cats that might have snitched on me, and when I found out it was going to be hell to tell the captain. So after questioning me and searching my car he found my .45 caliber gun under the front seat.

He also found a half pound of weed in the trunk, so he arrested me and took me downtown to the police station. They held me over night and I bonded out the next morning. Fuck, I got to get a punk ass lawyer because these pussy ass niggas hating, I thought. It was a Saturday morning. My head was still ringing from Major. He really fucked me up last night on the phone with the things he said. Maybe I was still more like him than I thought I was, and that's fucked up! I called up my girl and she answered on the first ring.

"Hey, baby, it's me." I said to her.

"Where were you last night?" she responded.

"In the hood."

"Doing what, that you couldn't pick up your phone?"

It's too early for this damn shit, I thought to myself. "Did you wake up on the wrong side of the bed or something?" I asked.

"No Kendrick and I know you were out there playing that K$treetz shit, acting a damn fool. I swear to God, sometimes I hate the hell out of you! All I ask is for you to call me every other day at the least, and you can't even do that. I mean you can call and leave a message on my machine saying that you been thinking about me or something."

She sounded fed up. All I could do was shake my head. "Damn! Well, what can I say?"

"I don't know! But I always stay up waiting on a call from you and it never happens. I'm in the Air Force trying to make a better life for us and you act like you just don't give a flying fuck! I bet you ain't checked your messages. Have you?"

"Naw."

"I know you didn't. So what you need to do, Ken, is check your damn messages to hear what I got to say to you and start calling me back whenever you get home or out them fucking streets because I'm busy right now."

I laughed and said, "Cool" before hanging up. I was too damn tired of arguing. Shit! If people only knew how much dumb stuff I went though.

I was flipping damn near a thousand dollars a week now and playing ball but still had problems. Life was a pinball game for your ass, and I still had to set up that bank account like Lamar, another cousin of mine, was telling me about. I needed that nigga Major, straight up! I didn't know what I was going to do without him. I was getting all kind of money now, and I didn't want to waste it.

Yeah, I knew exactly what I was going to do for Major's ass. I got this hookup on tickets for a cruise that I would give him when he get out. I listened to my voicemail and there were messages from earlier that day.

"Yo, Ken, this Prince, nigga. What's up? I mean are you trying to get some ass or what? Call me, and let me know what time it is. I got two bitches on deck."

BEEP! "Hey Ken, this is your big sister Jada. Look, me and Ramón are going down to Florida for a little winter getaway this weekend. I know you were talking to aunt Catharine about needing to just get away from it all. So call me back. We're leaving in the morning at 7:00am." Seven? Damn, it was already 10:00 a.m. They had been gone, I thought to myself.

BEEP! "You know, Kendrick, I'm real tired of this. I mean, maybe you trying to play me out like a hoe now, but then you wanna call me up out the blue and start talking that shit about how you love me and how you need me. I mean, it's confusing me, baby. What do you want with your life Ken? You can't just do one thing one day and some totally different shit the next day. You just end up running in circles.

Now look, I love you like crazy, and I got to be crazy with all these fine ass military guys running around down here while you up there throwing your dick around I know you are because people been telling me. Just don't get me know diseases. I'm out, but just remember that you were never there for me.

So when I mess around and turn into a damn lesbian don't say I didn't warn you. I love you too much to mess with a nigga right now but I still have needs of my own to be fulfilled. Anyways, call me when you've finished fucking them other bitches!!! I'm just sitting here in my bed teasing myself and its getting old. Well...bye, Ken." Really?

A call like this from Carmen I knew all she wanted was some attention and a few dollars. I sent $4,500 to Carmen that I'd just hustled up on. I was going back to Georgia where she lived so we could get a crib. The money was to buy new furniture, because I wasn't moving there to live on used and old furniture.

This one day stuck out. I called her phone and the number kept saying it was disconnected. I called up her cell phone as well and also was also disconnected. What the fuck is the deal? I just sent her ass money to pay the bills and grab some furniture. There was some shit up in the game.

Later I found out that during this time, while she was serving her time in the military, that she met an airman from Dallas, Texas. They hooked up and got married all while we were dating. I was doing some things that might have contributed to this happening but never in my wildest dreams did I imagine the ultimate betrayal from this woman. I had invested two and a half years in this relationship.

Sure there were some ups and downs in our relationship but that's stand true with all relationship. Therefore it seemed to be a normal situation to me.

So to confirm this I called my cousin down there who told me that he saw in the military news that she had gotten married to this top gun motherfucker. Yep, that's right. She had married this military nigga alright. I simply hung up on my cousin and sat there on the bed in shock over this mind blowing turn of events. My first thoughts were to go down to the base in Georgia to kill every muthafucker in sight but I knew they'd throw me under the jail messing with military personnel.

Within days I received more calls from close friends telling me about this shit and all I could do was lie and say, "Yeah I knew." I sat for weeks trying to figure out what I was going to do but I decided to just leave it alone. That shit had a nigga down for two weeks just stressing about what I wanted to do. Then one day I got up to shower, shave and get myself together but then I looked in the mirror and said, "Yep, the kid got played!"
Fuck it, my mode was always MOB, that's money over bitches because they breed envy! This was my time to get my ass off the bench and back in the game, back to making money full time and with a new determination. My cousin Major had hooked me up with this tall dirty muthafucker named Chi-Town. Chi-Town put his addiction before his hoes and the shit that took him years to build. He was a tall, thin man with a nappy beard and hat. Chi-Town stood about 6'4" and 165 pounds. He always wore a dirty, thin, jean jacket. Though he was dirty and had a slight odor, he still had mad hustle. This nigga could hustle anything, straight up.

They said this nigga was the man back in the day, from what I could recall Major telling me.

He was a big time pimp, but now he wasn't anything more than a fast talking crack head and his best years were behind him now. He did have a few hoes, still. I wasn't feeling him at first because I thought he was a hater now, but I needed his crib because he had a hot spot and we had gotten too big to be hustling on the street corner. "Gone get your rocks off youngsters," he would always say everyday offering his women to me and my crew when he didn't have any money or ran out of the drugs we gave him to rent his place. "Y'all in the game now youngster."

Chi-Town prepared his final sales pitch. "Treat yourself, don't cheat yourself. Look at her." We took a look at the frail, white woman in the room. She brushed her hair with her right hand while placing her left one on her hip in best attempt to look sexy. "She ready for y'all, youngsters. What y'all gonna do?"

"Where your other bitches at?" I asked.

"Them bitches is for dough, not for show, young pimpin." Chi-Town responded. Darius turned to Prince and said, "Fuck it, I'll do it." As Darius broke the $20 he held in his hand and gave half of it to Chi-Town. "Uh oh," Prince said as he slapped him on the back. "Lil' Dee, you found some balls huh boy?"

So we cut out leaving Lil Dee behind because I had to go scoop up my new ride, from the lot. After signing all that damn paperwork, it must've taken like two hours. But it was well worth the wait. Man, I can still remember driving with extreme caution as I crossed the intersection of 45th Street and Broadway.

Although I was incredibly excited about my newest purchase, and even more so about driving it, I knew that cat was about to hate seeing me behind the wheel.

I had just grabbed this 1995 Cadillac Deville from a used car dealer with a small lot on 49th Street and Broadway.

Even with the title registration and the car being in the name of my father, there would be no misunderstanding that the car truly belonged to me. My Cadillac was white with white and blue interior and Dayton rims.

My only thoughts were to roll through the hood and floss my shit. As I cruised up the block I pushed the power to my pioneer stereo system with the two six by nine speakers. Damn, I'm copping the sub-woofer ASAP, is what I was thinking. Meanwhile, I started looking through my CD book for Tupac's "All Eyes on Me." I quickly popped the CD in and played "Picture me Rolling." I then leaned back in my seat.

My manz and I started bobbing our heads to the beat. I pulled up right next to a crowd of girls standing in the intersection.

You know I had my hat cocked and my elbow hanging out the window, chin resting between thumb and index finger, and right hand clutching the wood grain steering wheel. I envisioned myself to be of the same breed of Cadillac driving, slick talking hustlers I had seen growing up and started to love as a young boy, plus some of my cousins and uncles were in this club also. The group of girls stepped closer to the Cadillac in hopes of getting a closer look at me. I accommodated them by looking in their direction. All the girls flashed their best 'I'm available' smiles as the light turned green and I coasted into the traffic.

"Damn, they are on it," Prince said as he peered through the back window at the teenage girls who still stood in the same spot watching attentively as I drove farther and farther away.

"You think they're on it, now, wait, till I get them sounds and that Cad grill," I said as I looked through the rearview mirror. Finally, I turned left at the intersection of 28th and Broadway. As usual, dozens of people lined both sides of the street. After allowing a procession of lesser vehicles to pass by, I pulled my shit across Broadway and directly toward the waiting crowd. As I leaned back farther in my seat I pulled alongside a group of 28th Street regulars that included Evelyn and Chi-town. "What'd up doe?" I said through the window as I rolled to a stop. "Where you been, pimping?" Chi-town said as he hurried toward the car. "I got customers."

"I've was buying my new wipe doc."

"Fasho, that's what it do, but we got money to make." Chi-Town said looking around.

"What you need?" I said as I grabbed a sack full of rocks from under my thigh.

"Hold on."

Chi-Town returned to the crowd. "That cat always on the grind," Prince said as we watched Chi-town collect money from everyone in the group except Evelyn. "I got $218," Chi said as he returned to the driver's side window.

Evelyn was standing two paces behind him. I arranged an assortment of various sized rocks in my hand and then gave them to Chi-town. "I love you, too," Chi-town said visibly excited by the amount of crack given to him.

"So what you think of the whip, Chi-Town?" I was slightly disappointed I had to ask.

"This your shit?" Chi-town said giving the Cadillac a quick look over.

"Fasho."

"That's a bad ass hog you got there, pimpin."

"That's what's up!" I added.

"Be careful, it's a lot of cats that don't like you around this city and will hate on you and your crew because y'all getting money," Chi-Town warned me before running back towards the restless crowd. "This yo' car, daddy?" Evelyn spoke seductively now that it was her turn at the window. "Yeah." I answered and smiled. "I bought it yesterday." "Oh, I like it too, daddy." Evelyn rubbed my chest.

"Wanna roll with me, later?" I asked her. Even though she was a smoker, I still considered Evelyn to be a very sexy woman. She was a bad older chick, about 5'6" and around 145 lbs. with brown skin, and a thick ass like a motherfucker. Damn, Evelyn was a hot dope head, I thought.

"You're just teasing like always," Evelyn said sounding disappointed.

"No, I'm not. I'll pick you up later, straight up," I promised her.

"Ok!" Evelyn handed me a few crumpled up bills. "I got $46, baby."

"Here." I reached inside the bag and gave Evelyn four $20 rocks. "You can pay me the rest later."

"How much I owe you?"

"We'll talk about it." As I released the brake leaving Evelyn to ponder my last statement, I turned the volume on the stereo as loud as possible while continuing my path down 28th Street.

Chapter 14

Everythang Workin'

Later that evening I got a call from Lil' Dee on my cell. I answered, "What's up, playboy!"

"Where y'all at?" Prince yelled.

"What's wrong?" I asked.

"Come to the Quality Motel," Darius instructed. "And bring some weed and drank, my nigga."

"What!"

"Look," Darius took a deep breath and attempted to compose himself. "I got three broads, four of 'em top notch. They wanna smoke and drank."

"Lil' Dee, you must be tricking," I said and then laughed in the phone.

"Big homie, please! These broads are all that. Get five bottles and bring some weed. We'll be in room 254. I'll pay you back."

I considered Darius's plea as I waved for Prince to come so I could fill him in on what his manz just asked me and to see if he wanted to go see these hoes with me. I know the type of bitches Darius thinks are fine. After I told Prince the details he was in. "Fasho! It can't hurt to go see what's up."
I called Darius back and let him know I was coming and asked what type of bottles he wanted. "See one of these hoes coming out of her clothes already," Darius said. "Fasho playboy, we on the way right now," I assured him.

"Don't be playing, nigga."

"We'll be there in 20 minutes, doc."

"I'm waiting on you." Darius added.

"These bitches better be as fine as you say," I let him know before I got off the phone.

Now, as I rolled slowly through the Quality Inn parking lot in search of room 254, I was certain that I made a bad decision fucking listening to Darius and coming here. Darius was joined by a white chick who was an average broad, blonde hair and blue eyes, nothing to call home to mama about.

Darius was shirtless sweating profusely and holding a half of bottle of gin. "Give me a $50," Darius ran up to the car saying. I was now irritated. "You didn't say shit about no crack! I know you ain't brought us all the way down here for some damn crack heads!"

"Told you, Ken," Prince shook his head.

"The hoes are inside." Darius threw the now empty bottle onto the pavement, breaking it beside my car. "All I was doing was holding the lick down until y'all got here." "Dig that, Darius," I said now trying to calm my lil' nigga down before he started getting more animated and bringing attention because he seemed to be very drunk. The woman took a step backwards as Darius flung both arms to his side and yelled even louder. "Every time I wanna do something, it's gotta be a motherfucking problem!"

"Cool out, Darius," Prince said as he got out the car. "Fuck that shit!" Darius was so furious that tears fell from his eyes. "Y'all act like everything I do is stupid or something. Y'all supposed to be my niggas!"

"I got some butter, fool. Stop it." I said as I jumped from the car and pulled out a big bag full of freshly cut cocaine rocks.

"And they got three. If y'all don't wanna kick it with me, just tell me, son," Lil' Dee was highly intoxicated. "It ain't like that Darius," Prince said as he stood at his drunk friend's side.

He placed his arm around Darius's neck and the two of them sat on the curb.

Darius bawled uncontrollably as I approached the frightened woman. "I heard you wanted some coca?" I asked her. She held the $100 dollar bill in my direction.

I then took the money from her and gave her two large pieces of crack cocaine. The chick smiled broadly, "I'll be back." She took off very quickly. I turned back to my crew. What a pitiful sight they were. Darius shoulders and 150 lb. frame shook violently as the big baby continued to cry. Meanwhile, the taller Prince continued his useless attempts consoling his grief stricken homeboy.

"Y'all supposed to be my manz," Darius repeated over and over between sobs. Unable to think of anything else that might quiet him, I reached through the driver's side window, pushed the lighter in, and waited for it to get hot. I then lit a square for him. "We are your manz, Darius," I said as I sat on the opposite side of him and tapped him on the leg while holding the square for him. He raised his head slowly and eyed the square momentarily before reaching for it. Once in his hand, Darius slowly and deliberately brought the square to his mouth.

He closed his eyes tightly while pulling softly on the square, causing the last of the tears to fall to the pavement. "I'll die for y'all, niggas," Darius whispered before taking a second puff from the Newport in his mouth. A door opened behind them, allowing the sound of rap music to become audible. I turned quickly. A bad chick stood in the doorway wearing red shorts and a white blouse.

"Y'all got another port?" the girl asked. Darius stood up quickly motioning with his head for the others to follow as he barreled toward the doorway.

Darius handed the girl the Newport before pushing her aside and entering the hotel room. "Y'all come on." The girl waved to Prince and I as she hit the weed. As I approached the room I began to bob my head to the music and rap along with Biggie's "Juicy". Another girl stood just inside the door.

She was petite with a fat ass. A pretty light skinned young chick who had on an oversized #34 Chicago Bears jersey. She smiled at me soon as I walked past her.

Once I entered the room, my mouth dropped at the scene before me. A large speaker was turned on its side while a thick, cinnamon colored broad, clad only in some lacy black panties danced on top of it. Damn, let's get this shit cracking, is what I was thinking. "Pop that thang, girl," Darius shouted while sitting on the bed next to the fourth young lady.

She was a shade darker than the chick that was on the speaker. She wore a pair of tight, fitted blue jeans and a solid black t-shirt. She had freshly done feet as she showed through the front of the open toed sandals she wore. Darius lit a blunt and gave it to her and slid the bottle of gin out of a cooler on the floor. He then grabbed three more 40 ounces of Colt 45 Malt Liquor and started filling cups up.

Darius then went back in to his pocket bringing the remainder of the weed I brought him out on to the table and began rolling two more blunts. He began to light one at a time and started passing them around, and mind you he already gave one to the chick seated on the bed.

Now there were four blunts rotating around the room stopping at everyone but me because I didn't smoke. I was speechless as I made my way over to the table to grab a cup of beer. I took the cup and began sipping it. I took a side step to my right so I could get a better view of the bitch on the speaker with the thick ass. "Ow, girl!" Darius sounded like Sir Mix A Lot, the rapper from back in the day, as he stood directly in front of the speaker and the dancing girl. I started laughing as the dancing chick bent forward allowing the jiggling mounds of flesh to slap against Darius's face.

"Darius was right this time." Prince said standing behind me long enough to grab a 40 ounce. I turned around to acknowledge my manz but I saw he had already cut out and returned to the two girls by the floor. The first girl was now sitting on the floor fanning herself with both hands while the second girl was pressing so hard against Prince that the two of them looked like Siamese twins. "OWWWWW girl!" Darius was having the time of his life.

His mouth was wide open now as the dancing girl continued to slam her generously proportioned breasts against his face. I stepped back as a tap on my left stole his attention. The chick on the bed reached for my hand while gibbering something about her name being Charmaine and driving from Orlando, Florida. I sat down next to her.

Without speaking, the girl took the weed from her mouth and placed it between my lips. I took a hit of the blunt as Charmaine took my hand and placed it under her shirt and firmly against her stomach. I hit the weed again and put it back in her mouth. I then checked out the room once more.

The hoe sitting on the floor continued to play with herself. Beads of sweat were running down her face. Prince and the chick wearing the Walter Payton jersey were stretched out on the floor.

She was on top of him. The broad on top of the speakers was now completely naked. Lil Dee was on his knees in front of her, both hands stretched outward, puffing vigorously on the blunt protruding from his mouth.

"Wanna fuck me, baby?" I heard a female voice asking me. As I turned back to the chick beside me, she was so close to me like she was my jacket. She then pulled the black t-shirt over her head and threw it on the floor. She then wiggled free from them jeans and kicked them aside.

She stood in front of me wearing only a dark green bra and panty set. "Wanna fuck this pussy?" Charmaine repeated. I nodded while taking a shot of vodka. This chick took my hand and put it in her panties. I slid my fingers towards that pussy as she put her fingers in her mouth and moaned. I played with her clit as she started moaning louder.

My dick began to get hard. "Press down hard on that clit, daddy." I pressed my index finger against her clit like she asked and rubbed her with the other ones. She then lay on her back and pulled me on top of her. She closed her eyes as I laid slowly on top of her, grinding my dick on her hot, wet pussy lips. "What are you doing to me?" I could hear someone say at the same time. It sounded like the girl on the speaker talking. "Oh God, this muthafucka is the best pussy licker ever!"

I looked up and then looked quickly back to the bitch underneath me as I continued to press my dick firmly against her pussy. "What the fuck are you trying to do to me?" The chick on top of the speaker screamed. Darius yanked her panties down and had her on the speaker as he stuck her ass out.

Saying nothing, he kneeled down and licked her pussy. She almost cried because of the pleasure he gave her. Meanwhile, Prince was with the other two bitches. The younger chick in the Payton Jersey started to have fun. First Prince and her started kissing the third girl together on the face then the neck.

Then they both wandered around from face to nipples to pussy. Then the girl in the jersey got on her hands and knees and started licking the dark skin chick pussy. As that was going on, Prince freaky ass started licking the bitch in the Bears Jersey.

Damn, it's going down in this bitch, I thought to myself. They finished it off with Prince fucking the dark-skinned chick from the back and the girl in the jersey was on his face. Wow, it was a great show but the best was yet to come. As I continued to rub my dick on this other chick she was going crazy. I could tell she was close to coming, and I hadn't even started fucking her yet.

It was later that night and I had been working these streets like a job. I had started shutting down my spots for the day. That's when I hit up Evelyn, a 40 year old crack head whom worked for me. We were driving around in my '95 Cad late that night to find a place to fuck her. On this particular night we had ended up right in front of her girlfriend's house in the driveway. It was 2:30 am and all the lights were off, so we started fooling around right there.

I started by playing with her beautiful, firm breasts and became hard right away.
Evelyn was not your average dope head. She was sexy as hell, 5'8," 34-26-36, long black hair with a phat ass, nice long legs, and brown eyes.
You would not have even known that she even got high by looking at her.
She leaned down and started sucking my shit. We both got real excited, and being that the Cad is a roomy car we reclined the front seat. I got on top of her and proceeded to open her legs and fuck the shit out of this old bitch. I made it very enjoyable because the whole time I was hitting it she was screaming, "Oh God, oh God, I'm coming daddy." Then she squirted everywhere. Now, that's what I call messy sex. After fogging up the windows and getting dressed again, we realized the lights were on in the house.

The front door was open, and her friend was sitting at the kitchen table, which was next to the door, which she was facing. From then on I had to give her a bump because she was threatening to tell Chi-Town. That was until one day I finally said, "Fuck it, tell the nigga. I'm not giving yo' ass shit else!" This nigga worked for me. He was an ex pimp. He knew how the game goes.

Evelyn and I would continue to fuck for a few more weeks until she caught feelings, on top of her catching a small drug case. This was a relief for me because I think I was catching feelings too. Damn, I was kinda open over the crack head chick, how is that possible? But after a short 60 day county jail vacation, Evelyn was back. Although this was my first run in with the legal system, Evelyn took care of that situation for a nigga by taking the rap. That showed me she was loyal and had my back. With the remaining drugs I had, I broke it up and let Prince be the distributor. I was shaken up by everything that went down, so I went back to refocusing on tightening up my basketball skills. I opened up a membership at the local YMCA and ran into a cat that was interested in me playing for a city league basketball team.

Chapter 15

Chasing Professional Dream'$$$

Have you ever been given a third chance to compete for your dreams? I had after not graduating from high school on time and acquiring my GED, on top of not being able to play basketball my senior year. And this was after making First Team All-State in my junior season and getting a scholastic to go to Bloomberg State College on a full ride only to get kicked because my teammates smoked weed in our dorm. I never got the opportunity to play one game at the university level. Now I was getting this third chance to play pro ball.

While some scouts came to seek out some other guys at a PRO AM tournament I was playing in, I wound up getting picked. I was one of the best in my city but was never seen by any pro scouts, but after moving to Maplewood I was now given a third chance when selected to play in a tournament to show everyone I could succeed in NCAA College Basketball and go to college.

Meanwhile on my way to becoming a street star, I meet this Mexican cat named Miguel Hernandez. At first I didn't think this guy was anybody but Miguel had an uncle that was the owner of the local professional team.

Miguel believed I was good enough to play for their team but he told me not to let my past get in my way of my future. Miguel and I really started to become good friends over the next few months. After the newly acquired friendship with him, Miguel asked me to play on a city league team.

I did it because Miguel was cool just so happened he was about to become vice president of basketball operations for the Panthers, his uncle's professional team. I also did it because he had the hottest nightclub in the city where I was VIP. While playing for Miguel on the city league team, we were 10-0 that summer and our team made it to the championship game. Miguel's uncle told him that if his team won he'd promote Miguel to the position he had asked for, so I knew I had to perform well. I was very nervous. At the start of the game I was sweating heavily and I knew it was just my nerves, but after they scored the first basket it was on. I came down the court and ran a pick and roll, passed it to my big man, and he scored just like that. The score was tied and I knew it was on then.

After the first quarter the score was 23-19 with us in the lead. I was playing great, having chipped in with 11 points, four assists, and three rebounds. By the end of the game I scored 44 points, 15 assists, and 11 rebounds. We won by 19 points. I knew Miguel was getting the vice president of player personnel job. I was about to get a new opportunity at being a professional basketball player and I was going to take full advantage of it. I played two seasons for the Maplewood Panthers. I wasn't a key player and sometimes I didn't even suit up, but I did receive a signing bonus of $7,500 and a paycheck at the end of each week for $1,400. Some games when we were up and down, I got in and did my thang in the short periods of playing time. I wore number 18, a number I picked as a kid if I ever made it to the NBA.

I decided to wear the number since I was now in the CBA. My first season I averaged 2.1 points a game, 1.7 rebounds, 2.2 assists, and 2.5 minutes. It was not what I imagined at all, but the CBA is all about what college you attended and the quality of your agent. Since I did not have an agent and I played junior college ball, I got a good dose of the bench. I thought I was better than most of the players that played ahead of me but I had no résumé. Never the less, I enjoyed every day with this team from the practices, games, bus rides, plane trips, hotel stays, everything. I really enjoyed the stories and thoughts from guys with NBA experience, the tales from their experiences overseas, anything about money, sex, games they played in, basketball players they played against, and tips on how I could get better at the game. I really appreciated my teammate's contributions during the first season in Maplewood. The first thing everybody told me was not to blow the $7,500 signing bonus on anything dumb. I wasn't even thinking about anything like that. I was just happy to be getting the opportunity to land a deal of this magnitude. I was making $45,000 for two years, with a chance to make $90,000 over that period.

One of the first things I wanted to do was get a new condo now that I was making some legit money. Then I wanted to make it through the full year, as well as the next one, because in the CBA there were no guaranteed contracts. You had to earn your money or you didn't get it if you weren't showing up to work or lacking in providing production. I was about 20 years old and just removed from the streets only because I was getting this second chance to live out my childhood dream to be a professional athlete. This was more than worth my while. During the first few weeks I developed a close personal relationship with one of my teammates, an older player and the starting point guard, A.J. Cheatum aka Cheetah.

He was one of the CBA's best players and also known for his cat like reflexes, athleticism, and his superior foot speed that gave him the ability to reach excessive speeds on the court. This made him close to unguardable, so nobody wanted to check him. He was only 5'8" and 168 lbs. but he could take over a game anytime he was ready.

We started our own private group called B.P.P., Ball Playing Pimps, and our mission was to see who could get the most and the baddest chicks. It really was competitive. We would go from state to state, city to city, and after every game we were on it, jack. The B.P.P. consisted of Cheat, Darius Grant, Courtney Strong, Keith "keeping coming back" Black, and myself. We went hard on and off the court.

Sometimes I would catch them trying to keep a secret log of the results. Much to the dismay of the others, I was in the lead. It had stopped being a competition to me because I was blowing them out the water, but I never told because I looked up to Fat-Cheat and always wanted him to think he was winning. I figured he could make or break my career.

One night after a 101-79 victory over the New York Lighting, most of the team was scattered throughout The Pines, a trendy nightclub near our downtown stadium, which the team owner Oscar Hernandez also owned. They were having a birthday party for our coach, Lawrence Hawkins.

It was his 50th birthday and we were celebrating a win. Cheat had played well again. He led us with 28 points and 11 assists. I hadn't played at all. Hawkins didn't have much faith in me because I was a rookie. Cheat and Keith thought that because I was not playing I would be distracted when it came to the contest we always had.

They should have known that I was always game, no matter what, because I had mad conversation when it came to talking to women. Cheat wasn't eager to convene a meeting of the B.P.P. in front of Hawkins. He knew he could do it on the sly since the birthday boy sat alone in the a far corner of The Pines nursing a ginger ale while lost in his own dark thoughts.

A former star player, Hawkins, was also a recovering addict who missed the halcyon days of cocaine and Wild Irish Rose, even though a formidable coupling of the two had on several occasions landed him in the slammer, and finally, in the 30 day, dry-out, $10,000 a week Richard Pryor Clinic. He emerged committed to sobriety, but he saw a far less interesting personality when pressed, friends had to agree.

The laptop sat unopened at his side. Hawkins still wrote out his game plans in long hand and his inability to open emails had once caused the team's internal system to crash. The gift was, as Hawkins saw it, another indication that Hernandez didn't really know him as well.

This was also a dead giveaway that the owner was on the board of directors of the computer company and got that damn thing for free. I also knew that coach didn't like me, not only because I was a rookie, but also because my other source of income was selling what had once held him captive for years.

I put that together because Hawkins drafted Cheat six years before me and Cheat was the starting point guard ever since.

Never the less, I was going to work my ass off to get my shot and prove that I belonged.

As the night went on I came across two fine ass ladies at the main bar. The women said they were "freelance models," though they were vague about their resumes. Cheat suspiciously thought that one of them looked like an enthusiastic supporting player in one of his pornos. At that moment I drained my fourth Heineken then asked the ladies if they wanted to take this party up to the VIP room upstairs.

Meanwhile, Keith Black, one of the team captains and members of B.P.P., started hating. He pulled me to the side and said the VIP room was off limits to rookies unless Oscar Hernandez requested for a particular player for a meeting, which had been the case on this night. "Dig that Playboy, well I'll take my party to my crib I'm out!!! Come on ladies…" In my head I was like why do I hang around these fucking clown-ass haters, but I quickly remembered I was trying to make it at this pro ball shit.

I'd do whatever it took to stay although kissing a little ass was not really me, but sometimes you just do what you have to do to make it in what you're trying to make it in!

It had already been a crazy night at the bar. It was right around 1:30 am when we got to my black Cadillac truck on them deuces. Upon our arrival to my condo gates I was really hoping that I was going to fuck both of these chicks. If I played my cards right a threesome was definitely going to happen.

Soon as we got in my front doorway, Devon started taking off her sheer white silk blouse, no bra, and black thong. She had that drunken "Come fuck me" look and she was ready for me. The other chick, Lexus, had already made her way to my living room and sat on the couch. Out the club and in better lighting, Lexus was simply stunning with brown eyes and shoulder length, black hair.

Devon on the other hand was a black brunette with blond streaks and green eyes that had to be contacts, but both of these bitches were hot. Lexus and Devon then disappeared into my kitchen to round up some more drinks for us. As they reappeared with the drinks they started kissing a long, wet, French kiss. Wow, this caught me off guard completely, but damn if it wasn't a beautiful sight. As they broke the kiss I could see that Devon's nipples were as hard as they could get, sticking through the silk blouse. Lexus also displayed very hard nipples.

They then started rubbing their tits against one another's. My dick was rocked up! Devon asked me, "Is this what you want to see?" I replied, "HELL YEAH!" With that, both of these sexy bitches sat down on each side of me and kissed again. "Would you like to fuck him together?" Devon asked Lexus.

"Oh Yes!" Lexus responded.

Devon then reached down to undo my belt and zipper on my pants. As Devon pulled out my dick, Lexus also reached down to feel my length and commented, "Damn, that's a big ass dick and I can't wait to suck it." Meanwhile, I was busy getting both girls' blouses unbuttoned to fondle their rock hard tits and find the wetness between their legs.

I put my fingers into both of their hot pussies as they finished undressing me and then found each other's lips again. Both women were also finding each other's pleasure zones with their hands and tugging at their nipples.

Lexus and Devon both went down on my dick and took turns running their hot tongues on both sides and the head. With all that had gone on to this point I could not help but to cum into both of their waiting mouths. I filled Lexus's mouth until she came off my dick, then I filled Devon's mouth with my white, hot lava. Both swallowed my nuts and then exchanged another lip assault swapping my cum between them.

They both agreed that my load was the best tasting ever and went back to sucking me back hard. Then they both looked up and said they were still horny for my dick. Devon asked me if I could make Lexus come. I positioned myself between Lexus's open legs and started licking her pussy while Devon went to work sucking Lexus's hard nipples and kissing her.

Lexus was enjoying the licking I was giving as she reached up and moved Devon's thong aside to find her hot box dripping wet. I could hear Lexus's fingers sliding in and out of Devon's pussy, and from my vantage point I could see the wetness on Lexus's hand.

Devon was tweaking both of her nipples with her thumbs and forefingers. I decided to insert my fingers into Lexus's wet little pussy as I ate her and increased the pace of my tonguing.

All of a sudden Lexus started to quiver and cum. She was telling me she was going to cum and then started gushing her liquids out on to the couch. Yes, Lexus was a squirter.

This was the first time I had ever been with a women who ejaculated. What a beautiful sight. Her orgasm was so wet and intense.

Devon saw what was happening and said that it was ok and that she had made Lexus cum earlier by her hand when they were getting dressed to come to the party for my coach. With that Devon went down on Lexus's tits licking and sucking while I ate Lexus to another sensational climax.

Devon watching Lexus cum stroked her own clit and she came with Lexus, both women feeding off the moans and cries of each other. Lexus again came on the couch. I then moved up and positioned myself behind Devon to fill her with this dick. Lexus was in the position to fondle my balls as I entered Devon. Devon instantly came again as I fucked her deeper than she'd ever been fucked before from behind. As Devon came she found Lexus's mouth and I reached around to rub her clit driving Devon to another one of her multiple orgasms.

I busted again inside Devon and as I did I pulled my dick out to cum on Lexus's face and chest. I shot on to her beautiful tits and then spanked the sides of her mouth with my dick in an effort to get every drop out for these women to enjoy. Lexus was rubbing my cum around her hard nipples and Devon lapped every last drop up.

Meanwhile, the rest of my cum oozed from her hot pussy hole. Devon then looked up at me and told me that they said that they would make it worth my trip and time for leaving the club early.

"Listen Ken, I want to watch you fuck Lexus," Devon said. I then positioned myself over Lexus and Devon stroked my dick and glided it into Lexus. As I started slowly fucking Lexus, Devon rubbed my back and then started to playfully slap my ass.

Devon asked me if I thought Lexus was beautiful. My response was, "Hell yes." I could feel Lexus's pussy gripping my dick as she started to fuck me back riding in rhythm.

"I love to see another woman getting fucked by a long dick, ebony man. Now y'all making my fantasies come true." Devon said as she began to play with herself. "Now Ken, you fuck Lexus hard like you fucked me."
Devon then lay down beside us as I grabbed Lexus behind her knees and placed them on my shoulders as I pounded her pelvic bone. While I was starting to break a sweat, Devon was stroking herself to yet another orgasm. With one last thrust we all came together and fell into a coma like sleep. That was one hell of a night.

Hernandez had owned the Panthers for about four years and Hawkins has been with the franchise all of the years he had owned the team. Hernandez was a self-made millionaire that got rich from an Internet company he started where you could get anything for under $10.00. He sold it at the right time and struck gold with his profits.

He always loved profession basketball on top of it had never been a Mexican owner before. I finished the season off, after a 4-2 playoff loss to the St Louis Cardinals. I ended the year with an average of 1.3 points, 1.5 assists, and 0.7 rebounds.

I played one more season in the CBA and in this one I was just filling the roster and collecting checks. I didn't get any playing time. Half way through that season I got cut for Master P the famous rapper.

So back to the block I went full time. I opened up two spots up on the east side and everything was working. I did continue to work out and managed to play pickup basketball.

Chapter 16

Can't Win for Losing

I played on this tour team called The Italian Red Wolves where I got $5,000 plus $200 a week while we were there to play 20 games against the foreign national teams to get them ready for the upcoming Olympics. They had ten tryouts with 250 people at each of them, and I was one of the 18 players they selected to go to Italy.

The training and workouts were hard as hell, but it was basketball so it was what it was, you know. After two months of practicing and preparing it was four days before our plane left for Italy. I was about to shoot to my hometown to see my family and friends before I left for Italy. This rather good looking woman was walking up to people at the local self-serve gas station next to the interstate asking everyone for "Gas money." As she approached me, she told me her sob story of running away from an abusive relationship and she stated that she was totally broke and "Depending upon the kindness of strangers." I asked her how well it was working and she told me that it was pretty bad.

I offered her a business opportunity. I had $50 set aside for sex and I was willing to give it to her if she fulfilled my need. She laughed and said she wasn't that type of girl but thanked me for the offer and proceeded to ask others at the station for cash. I finished pumping my tank full, I noticed that she was still penniless and asking the last few people around for cash. This time as she approached again, she opened by saying.

"Why does a guy like you have to buy it anyway?"

"I don't like to feel obligated to a woman. I really just like anonymous recreational sex," I responded.

"Ok, what if I say yes? Will you give me a ride back here?"

"Better than that, we can do it here."

She was somewhat reluctant, but a few minutes later I was following her through the outside men's rest room door and had some of the hottest sex ever. She wore a knee length dress and white sheer to waist stockings, complete with g-string thong panties underneath and a pair of one and a half inch conservative black heels. I lifted her skirt, rolled her hose mid-thigh and untied her thong panties on one side. I first probed with my finger, finding that she was tight and wet with one of the finest shaved bushes I'd ever seen.

We did it doggy style with her holding onto the sink watching me in the mirror as I pumped her tight pussy full of my dick. I sprayed sperm deep into her pussy as I probed her asshole with my index finger of one hand and rubbed her clit with the other. She stayed in position as I jacked myself hard again and pumped her asshole full of my nut too. It was heaven and the best $50 I'd ever spent. I can't lie I did exchange numbers with her.

She said she had just gotten out of a bad relationship plus the pussy was good. Right after that I walked back to my truck and peeled out with a smile on my face.

Following a week stay in Springfield I was off to JFK Airport for my 13 hour flight to Verona Italy. I couldn't wait until we touched down. I was starting to get air sickness.

During the first weekend there I was working out at a public fitness center in Italy during graveyard shifts. Some of the local players told me that it was normally pretty quiet but there was a bar a couple doors down. A lot of people from that bar parked in the same garage, and when the bars let out you'd sometimes have some problems getting out of there.

This one night, after finishing my workout I showered up and went down by the street at the entrance of the bar. I had to keep an eye on everything. That's when a trio of gorgeous chicks staggered into view on the way to their car in the garage. Two were fucked up and I guess the third was a designated driver or something but they were all sexy as hell.

One was a short blond girl with beautiful features and huge ass and tits. She looked like she was ready to fall out of her dress. She started coming on to me as soon as they got within earshot. I could smell the liquor on her but she started rubbing up against me real tightly as the other two watched and laughed. She then whispered into my ear that she wanted to give me a blowjob so I pulled her over into a stairwell.

She dropped to her knees and pulled out my dick, licking and sucking on it as I leaned back against the wall. I was thinking, "Damn, I love Italy already."

Finally I couldn't take it anymore and I pulled her up to her feet before digging a Magnum condom out of my wallet.

She was giggling as I pulled the rubber on and then lifted up her dress pushing my dick in her with all I had. She wrapped her legs around me as I pulled the top of her dress down to nibble on her lovely breast. I came within minutes and so did she. Then she left me there gasping as she pulled up her dress and went back outside to meet her friends. I never saw her again but for the next few days I did go to that fitness center hoping she'd come back again.

While in the first practice I was shooting a three pointer and one of my teammates put his hand up and came down with his finger going in my eye. After my feet touched the ground I couldn't do shit but think I just had lost my eye. I had never been as scared about something in my life.

I fell on the court in search of my eyeball. The pain was so excruciating that I really thought I'd lost it. The team doctors ran to the floor and were checking me out. It seemed the whole place just stopped. It felt like hours in those few minutes.

Meanwhile, after getting me to the hospital and in stable condition they told me I wasn't insured there in their country and they did all they could do for me. Right after I put on a profanity exhibition the team promoter came in the room with a first class ticket back to the states.

All I could think at that time was "Wow, fucking wow." This was the longest 13 hours in my life. I had my chick Olivia pick me up from JFK Airport and take me straight to the emergency room.

After seven hours of surgery with eight stitches and these yellow tinted glasses that I had to wear for the next two and a half months I was good to go.

For that money I was promised, I received $1,700. Fifteen hundred went to the New York City Hospital and $200 for gas to get home. What a life chasing these professional dreams. I had an opportunity to travel to a place I'd never image going to and due to the eye injury never got the chance to get the full experience.

After months of working out, rehab, and mad visits to the ophthalmologist, I landed a spot on the Kansas City Tornado's, the local ABA professional basketball team. We played our home games at Smoky Hill River Coliseum.

It was a physical league, full of players that had played all over the world in several different levels. The ABA was a fun, fast paced league but it was twice the war. Every week I took a shoulder or two under my chin that brought jelly to my legs.

See don't let the ABA fool you, there was tough competition every game. The ABA basketball game was a world in itself. You had to learn a few rules, the best players, and the lingo. The rules weren't hard either. The first rule was Big Melvin. Melvin was 7'0", 27 years old, close to 315 pounds, and he had volume. Whatever he said went because he would yell louder and longer than anyone else. He was the Shaq of the ABA.

Wayne Hughes was a 6'5" do it all guy with major jumping ability. Wayne was the best all-around player when I joined the league that was until after the first week of the season. In three games I was averaging over 30 points and 8 assists on top of being named the ABA player of the week, but that was not surprising.

I had played professional ball before, though I climbed to the top of the league within my first campaign obtaining another scoring title, all-star appearance, and taking my team to the ABA finals. I still found myself unemployed due to the nonguaranteed contracts and nobody wanted to sign me because they all thought I'd want a big money deal. So I went back to Springfield, worked out and helped prepare Kendall for college.

One day after coming home from a pickup run, recreational basketball, I had a missed call with a voicemail message from a number I didn't know.

So before calling the number back I listened to the message: ***"This message is for Kendrick Mackelmore. I am Adam, the head coach of the Gary Indiana Blue Jays here in the IBL. We are very interested in signing you to a three-year deal. Please call me back at your earliest convenience. My number is 765-574-3119."***

I was excited as heck, so after listening to the message for a second time I called Coach Adam back. We had a wonderful conversation and I went to meet with him and the owner to sign my new contract. I guess you could call me the IBL Michael Jordan or Magic Johnson because I, too, had done what they did on my level. See I was a three time all-star, scoring champ, and I won three titles in the three years I was in the IBL. I can remember the first one like yesterday. As I looked down at my watch, I couldn't help but notice that I only had 30 more minutes until my shift was over at work. However, the 30 minutes dragged at a snail's pace making it appear as though it were hours.

Continuing to stare at my watch minute after minute, I quickly was overcome by memories of my championship basketball game. My ears heard the sound of my watch tick each minute but my eyes were focused on my feet and arms that were moving uncontrollably. The victory of a vigorously challenging basketball game took place last Tuesday evening. With only five seconds left on the shot clock, my team was only down by one point. Those five seconds would determine who won the game if any point was scored.

Knowing this, I quickly dribbled the ball carefully with my left hand securing it as if it were my first born, while my right hand was well prepared to shoot over a defender. As I glanced at the shot clock, there was only three seconds until the game was over. It was in those three seconds that I felt as though God was on my team's side. Out of nowhere, a player who was defending me tripped and fell ass first onto the court's wooden floor.

The game began after the tip off. I was absolutely focused and determined to win this game. The butterflies within my body had disappeared. Ten minutes into the game, my body was already feeling the pain, but I did not care. I waited too long for this moment. I felt as though I was giving 110% in playing this game but my team was still down 20-26. Our opponents surpassed our expectation. They were a strong team much more potent than any of the teams that we had challenged. Just by staring into their big brown eyes, I could tell that they were just as determined as our team to win this game.

It is not a surprise that this team made it to the finals because they definitely carried strong players. Nonetheless, only one team was going home with the trophy and the bragging rights, ostentatiously. Thus, I was playing with all my might. I was not giving up without a fight. At the end of the game I can proudly say that it felt great to host my first professional championship trophy. It was the first of three, but still probably the best one of them all.

Gabriella Rivers, thick brown skinned beautiful ebony female with short hair, was just a sweetheart. We actually kicked it, or messed around, in high school, but we hadn't seen one another in years. One night we happened to run into each other at the gas station. She just so happened to be coming from the club that night and I had just made it into the city from Indiana.

I stopped because it was a gang of people at the gas station, so I decided to be nosey. As she was walking in the door before me, I kind of thought she looked familiar but you know how it is when you haven't seen a person in years. Then she turned around and that's when I realized it was her.

"What's up, Gabriella? How are you doing? Damn, you still looking good as ever," I said.

"Thanks, you are too. How long has it been? About five or six years, right?" she responded.

"Yeah something like that. Well damn, can a nigga get a hug or something?" As we got out of line and moved towards the door we gave one another an embrace that I'll never forget. It was not a nasty or disrespectful one either; just a good passionate hug that told that we had a past history if you were walking by.

After that great hug she said, "You should walk me to my car. I got my girls in the car with me. We just left the club. It was Jessica's birthday, that's the only reason I'm out."

"No doubt, I can do that if your man not going to get mad. I don't want to get anybody angry with me." She looked at me and we both had a good laugh.

"Boy, I am single and I can talk to anybody I please to talk too."

"Excuse me, Miss Independent." We laughed again.

"So, who are you dating or are you married?" she asked me. I let out a good laugh.

"I'm waiting on you to say yes!" I responded.

"Man, yup you still got good game but I ain't a teenager anymore."

"I was digging you then and I'm still digging you now, so what's up? You're single, I'm single we're not kids anymore so what's really good?"

"Look, I ain't trying to break up this little lovers reunion and all but a bitch hungry and got to get something to eat before all the restaurants close!" Tammy interrupted from inside the car.

"Okay Tammy I'll let y'all go when Gabriella exchange numbers with me so we can continue our conversation then." That's when Tammy gave shouted out Gabriella's number and ended the sentence with,

"Now let's go!" We all laughed as I asked if her friend giving me the number was ok and if I could use it. I then asked for another hug, which she gladly obliged by giving me another genuine embrace almost as good as the first one.

I always had a real thang for this woman and something inside me was telling me that it never left either. She then got in her car and pulled off heading north to where all the restaurants were still open. I walked toward my truck and heard my name being called. It was one of my niggas from back in the day. His name was Hakim but everybody called him "Sweet", a name that I gave him back in elementary school.

"What's up, my nigga? When you get in town?" asked Sweet.

"I just got off the highway about 30 minutes ago," I responded.

"Right, right, so I know you got that bag with you, don't you?"

"I got a little something with me, doc, why? What up? What you trying to do?"

"Like a four and a half pack," Sweet said.

"No doubt, I got you. Take my number, playboy, and hit me up in the morning. We'll do breakfast or something," I suggested.

"Bet, I'll get with you in the AM then."

I then walked away, got in my truck and sat in the truck reviewing what just happened. There was one small thing I left out. There was this dark skinned, baldhead cat that I knew.

I never fucked with dude before but he was sitting on the passenger side of Hakim's car. The funniest part was back in the day this nigga was a jack boy, and out of the blue Hakim called me over to his car with this cat in the ride with him talking about work. Just as I was thinking about my strange but wonderful meeting with Gabriella, my phone started vibrating on the center console. I looked down and it was Gabriella's phone number. I got excited to be getting a call so soon. I quickly got myself together and answered the phone.

"Hello?"

"Hey, this Gabriella."

"Yeah, I know because I never forget numbers I need to keep."

"See there you go with the good game again." We both shared a laugh. "But naw, seriously, I was just thinking about you though."

"Oh, yeah and if I may ask, what were you thinking Mr?" "Just that I was hoping this time we capitalize on this opportunity of making something happen unlike when we were teenagers."

"Yeah, I can understand that. I guess we will have to see how it goes."

"No doubt. So what's new with you these days?" I asked.

"Well as you know, I'm single and I have a son that's one year old. I work at this factory call N.A.D., North American Distributors. We make airplane parts. I've been there for like three years now," Gabriella updated me.

"Dig that."

"So what about you, Mister?"

"Well, I've been chillin'. I played pro ball in Indiana for the last two years. I have a daughter that's one and a half and that's about it with me." I wanted to tell her the rest but how can you tell a good woman that you are also one of the major violators of the Midwest. Believe, after a few dates and outings, Gabriella and I decided to make things official.

154

She and I had history. That's why we were able to pick up like that. It seemed meant to be. Within months of our relationship things couldn't have been better. I was back Springfield and I'd rekindled a relationship with a beautiful woman that I had so much in common with. It was time to get back to work. I opened up a YMCA membership and got back to the grind. I had a woman now so I had to keep a job now because I couldn't go back to the streets. I hadn't completely left them but I wasn't all in.

I was unable to make the cut on a CBA roster after seven years of hard work and determination, although I had been an ABA and IBL super-star. I was a good player but I was starting to question, if I had what it took. On top of my new found struggle to get ahead and obtain another good paying basketball job. So one of my homeboys I played summer league with who was balling overseas told me about all the weak players getting mad money over there. I knew I was better than him and had to hear how he was still playing pro for money in Spain after all these years. I was close to quitting basketball completely, until Gabriella told me how I should think about playing ball overseas again.

As I pondered over this situation, I decided to call my old teammate from back in CBA who was playing basketball overseas in China and getting paid over $300,000 a year. If that doesn't sound like a good career, I don't know what does!

"Hello?"

"What's up Black, this Ken!"

"What's up my dude, long time no hear."

"Yeah I know, right? But yo, I talked to Cheat and he told me you were playing in China now."

"Yeah I've been over there for like two years now."

"Dig this, doe doc, I'm trying to get a workout."

"No doubt, I'll see what I can do."

"But check it, though, most of these teams don't even know who I am. Will they be willing to sign me to play ball overseas?"

"Look Ken, you've put together a nice résumé and you're one of the best point guards I've seen. Seriously, now, you have the best chance of being noticed by overseas scouts. See the great thing about playing basketball overseas is that you can gradually improve your skill levels and still have many opportunities to join the NBA later on."

"That's what's up doc. I appreciate that."

"But one of the things I can't stress enough about getting into overseas basketball is preparation.

This is one of the key elements that 90% of players fail to do, which I know you're not in that category."

"No doubt if I take a workout I'll definitely be ready! I've been playing in the IBL and summer basketball leagues. Also I'm continuing my running and training drills. Also, playing pickup ball has been a great way to prepare myself for future tryouts and overseas scouts."

All over the world people of all ages dream of playing basketball professionally and making that all important career choice that keeps them financially set for life. However we all know that this dream doesn't always work out and that the majority of players will never get the opportunity to play for a professional team.

That brings me to this point. Black came through for me and got a few scouts to come check me out at one of our final IBL games. I had been playing basketball ever since I was one year old but this was only the second time that my team had made it to the finals while playing pro ball. On top of that, there were scouts there to watch me. Seven years later I finally got to live this dream, but I was enjoying every moment of it.

After actually talking to Black and getting my last chance to play ball, I was now thinking about going in a different direction. I repeated to myself over and over again, "Just one more game to go, just one more game to go!"

This final IBL game took place inside a local community recreation center, however the atmosphere in that venue had everything that one would want to have leading into a big time finale. The bleachers were full of screaming fans. Some family and friends crowded in the massive gymnasium, a basketball court as big as the NBA's best. It had all of the sights and sounds with a booming pep band in the back and hot cheerleaders and dancing girls calling out cheers in the front keeping the crowd hype.

While putting on my uniform I reminded myself that this was the last organized basketball game that I will ever play. Next year basketball would have to take a backseat because I would be occupied with working and adjusting to transforming from chasing this basketball dream into the reality of a regular workforce.

From the locker room I could hear the loud music being played over the PA system by the deejay and I was constantly reminded of the many times I walked into my high school or CBA games. Though I played well, actually winning the MVP, I sat in the locker room and looked back on my basketball career with a sense of excitement and release. These emotions of melancholy were running inside of me at the same time. Being pro athletes, we are blessed to be in a unique situation that puts us in a category that a small number of people will ever be part of.

At moments this standard of living can get lonesome, frustrating, depressing, and if you're not careful, especially dangerous. If you do go about it the right way, using basketball to travel the world can be an awesome experience. So when I came out the locker room and saw all the people that still remained in the gym. I saw the scout my boy Black sent coming straight toward me.

"Hey Kendrick, right?"

"Yes sir."

"I'm Bill, Bill Hanes international scout. I just wanted to say I think you have the skills to make it overseas."

"Thanks, sir!"

"Here's my card call me when you're ready to sign a deal."

"No problem, sir."

Even after getting that great news deep inside of me I knew I was ready to hang this hoop dream up. I ended up making what might have been the worst decision ever by not calling Mr. Hanes and not following up with his offer. In a real sense, I saw that my basketball dreams just were not going to happen.

I did not want to take a chance of going somewhere and not being successful again in a foreign country, not knowing the language, not knowing anyone, and being thousands of miles away from home and having the possibility of just being cut anyway. My spirit just could not take another disappointing blow. Therefore, I decided to return to something that I knew, and I was getting better and better at doing. Deep in my heart I felt I had reached the end of my rope. I was tired mentally, psychologically, and even more importantly, my body wasn't physically wanting to go through all that I needed to do to get prepared for another season's run.

Once again, I felt myself going back to the hustling game. I said "damn" to myself as I picked up my cell and called my cousin Major.

Summary

This is a story about the evolution of a young African American male and the trials and tribulations he faces while evolving into adulthood. I feel this story comes from a different angle, because the character doesn't come from the typical scenario of an urban beginning with a single mother, single father, grandparents raising him or alcoholic/drug addicted parents. He actually comes from a middle class, African American family where both parents do well but he ventured off track because of his own poor choices. It all begins with an innocent, young, African American teenager around age 13 or so and his love for sports, especially basketball, during the 80's.

Kendrick will have some great moments in high school as he quickly turns into a superstar athlete in three different sports, but these moments weren't just on the playing fields and arenas, either. With all his instant success came adversity that would deal him a life altering experience that shattered him beyond repair, but unlike most urban young men and women, he had family members all over the country he could travel to when he needed a getaway. Just like that he got a chance to travel to California along with two of his younger cousins. In typical Kendrick fashion, while out west he got an amazing opportunity but was not ready for it and ran from the possibilities. There came a time where the young man's dreams just seemed to fade away and something had to give, because he needed money to live. So on cue, like in a movie, he started gravitating toward the streets and the dope game. This young man had ambition, as well as the desire to be the best hustler he could.

The competitiveness from sports transformed him into the ultimate street hustler that had to put his name in the game. For most people luck only strikes once, and sometimes never, but Kendrick was the complete opposite. From a hood endeavor arose this professional basketball deal, so now he tries to balance basketball as well as the street life. Which will prevail?

After Kendrick jumped off the porch there was no turning back as he chased money, basketball, and women, equally. He did it from city to city, as well as state-to-state, with his mentor and big cousin Major, one of the most legendry Midwest hustlers. Major helped elevate Kendrick's street game to another level like a great coach with his superstar player as he molds him into a magnificent leader. Now that he's gotten to his peak you can see that he was a born leader as he put together his own teams and started making his name in the streets. He went from grabbing ounces to kilos and making his mark in the dope game. With the departure of Major he had to assume the position and be the HNIC. For people who don't know, that's Head Nigga In Charge.

After being groomed for the spot Kendrick would excel as he held the block down for his big cousin's absence. Kendrick didn't want to just do well, but he wanted to exceed Major's mark on the game, so he formed an all-female hustling team that over a short period of time put up extraordinary numbers. With any good run, though, they all come to an end so he had to make a choice to run or stay. He begins to see ain't no love in these streets, so change had to come and come fast.

Acknowledgement

To all those who provided support, talked with me, read, wrote, and offered comments, for those who allowed me to quote their remarks and assisted in the editing, proofreading, and graphic design of this book, I would like to express my sincere heartfelt gratitude. Thank you for your support.

This book was written to share the life and times of an urban youth who I have encountered personally, either by their stories or some personal experiences. This book has great characterization, and was written to teach many about the experiences I have had and shared with the reader and provide an opportunity to get some things off my chest. In writing this book it has taken me on an amazing journey down memory lane. I share this work with plenty of emotions in it. There are many characters in this book that were created based off of people who have supported me in this life: Bernard Johnson, Terrell Jefferson, Jerry Neal, Donzell Neal, Burnis Johnson, Jacarri Neal, and a lot of family as well as friends. Then I like to give a shout out to Jerry Neal, Donzell Neal, Melvin Lars, Franklin Fudail, Anita McKenzie for chipping in and helping keep me inspired and motived.

In the creation of this book I must first give thanks to the Almighty God who gave me energy, strength, and the focus needed to complete this task. For the guidance, assistance, and support in helping me, I want to express my appreciation to my mother, Carolyn Neal, my father, Stanley Neal, my brother, JaCarri Neal, and my close personal friends for their support in this endeavor. Without any hesitation, I want to thank my loving and supporting family of JaKeita Haire and Jawan Neal II, who have encouraged and supported me in spite of all the time it took me away from them and our lives. It has been long and very a difficult, challenge but also an enlightening learning experience for me. I want to give a special thanks to my writing and editing team of Shanika Carter and Malcolm Stevens for their help in enabling me to put this book together. And also my artist DeAnthony Carter for the great covers design, along with Vikki Hankins my Consultant. We know sometimes that with the best intentions we may forget, omit, or just do not include everything and everyone. To that end, please forgive me if I left anyone out. Just know I got you in the next book, Volume II 'Trappin' is Habit.' See you at the top!

March 24, 2014

Jawan Neal

iography

n R. Neal was born on
16, 1977 and raised in
egon, MI. He is the son of
lyn and Stanley Neal. He is the oldest
o boys. Being the oldest child, came
great pressure as well as responsibility
 an example for his young brother. It's funny because no one would
 known he was a writer nor like to creatively write, because of his
tic gifts. As a young man he wrote a short story about this basketball,
n the court off the court thinks that Professional players face which he
 'Ballers'. He never told or showed a soul. And the crazy thing about it
somebody created a similar show called 'The Game' a BET award
ing sitcom. It was then he knew he wanted to become an author. With
ush and support from close family and friends he decided to write his
tional novel 'Walk Witt Me' Volume-1, of a 3 part series.

n is currently a manager at a rental own company for the past 5 years.
as always want to write a movie his whole life and it is so fitting that
all the things he has done life has brought him back full circle and he's
g the opportunity to create a novel at this stage of his life is
omenal. I see that success is right around the corner for Jawan now that
 following a passion that no one even knew he had for telling these
nal stories. And like all other things he's perused in his life, I know he's
ng to win. A few quotes I'll leave you with:

"Keep the faith... And that the best is yet to come. Keep the faith that the next extraordinary version of you is being crafted even right now. Nothing can stray you from keeping your commitment to achieving your goals set for today and for the future. Strive for greatness! Keep the faith. Move forward in spite of your fears and despite any evidence to the contrary. Believe that IT'S POSSIBLE!!"

"I strongly believe if you're good at something, you owe it to yourself to purse it!"

"Always think positive thoughts because your thoughts become your actions. Remember to keep your actions positive because it is your actions that become your behavior. Always keep your behavior positive because your behavior becomes your habits. It's important to keep your habits positive because your habits develop your values. Maintain positive values because your values become your destiny. The choice is your, it's easy. Dream big stay positive, focus, and faithful..."

~ Jawan Neal ~

www.ingramcontent.com/pod-product-compliance
Lightning Source LLC
Chambersburg PA
CBHW060120260626
47160CB00005B/1947